Rubies of Ambition

Published by: Reading Stones Publishing
Helen Brown & Wendy Wood

Cover Design: Wendy Wood
Photo Credits:
Models Photo: Carpe Noctem Photography; Jennifer Maybury
Background photo, taken by Mitchell Plumbe, is of Boxing Glove Cactus (*Cylindropuntia fulgida var. mamillata*) located in far west NSW.

For more copies contact the Publisher at:

Glenburnie Homestead
212 Glenburnie Road
ROB ROY NSW 2360
Mobile: 0422 577 663
Email: hbrown19561@gmail.com

Gems of Australia
Faith Series
Book 2

Rubies of Ambition

Olwyn Harris

Dedication:

For Kathryn, who has always been my little actress... may you continue the journey towards fulfilling God's sparkling ambitions for you.

1

"I wish you would dress up. It'll be fun!" sighed Andi despairingly, looking at her friend's jeans. She always wore jeans. Jo calmly inspected her friend's costume. Andi looked every bit the nineteen-twenties' dancer. She had on a "flapper" drop-waisted dress, beads everywhere, headband complete with feathers. She was just shoving her long feet into low-heeled shoes. Andi stood up dramatically and did a rather poor rendition of the Charleston across her bedroom floor.

Jo gave Andi one of those quizzical "you've-got-to-be-kidding" looks. "I said I would come to the movie… but there is no way I'm going to put that stuff on. Your hair's wrong you know."

Andi grimaced as she grabbed her dark hair and tried to twist it up above her neckline. "I've tried all sorts of things - but it doesn't work." She glanced enviously in the mirror at Jo. "You easily pull off the twenties… why don't you try something a little more…?"

"I have a fedora and braces. This is a far as I go."

"Well at least you're coming," she conceded. "You don't mind really – do you?"

"You owe me. Big time," said Jo without hesitation,

peeling open one of her favourite chocolate bars. Andi decided then that she should drop it, or Jo could back out completely.

This latest whim of Andi's started when she heard the heritage listed *Roxy Theatre* was reopening for the cultural celebration week. She was fascinated right from the start. They were running a film festival of black and white, silent movies. She borrowed books from the library and read about the 1920's. This was the time when the whole world was relieved the Great War was over, and it seemed they were very determined to party. Life became a frenzied attempt to enjoy the celebration of living instead of existing between death and destruction.

Andi looked over the program and chose a movie called "The Daughter of Shiraz", starring Lillian Browning. The movie-star journals hailed Browning as one of the glamorous emerging Australian actresses, a star of the silent film era. Andi saw her picture on a poster print advertising "The Daughter of Shiraz". Her long lashes and wide mouth seemed poignantly sad. When Andi found they were screening the film on the anniversary of its opening night, Andi absolutely had to be there.

"The Daughter of Shiraz" sounded dramatic and romantic. Even though it was a corny old movie, the costumes and the era were captivating. This movie was about a Persian princess who tries to escape an arranged marriage by going to a modern university to learn diplomatic studies. She is naïve about the ruthless western city culture and is robbed of everything she owns. But rather than confess her shame to her family, she works as a dancer to support herself. She falls in love with the theatre, *and* the handsome, talented director – of course, even though he is poor, and the bankers have threatened to close him down. Just when they are getting a show together that will save the theatre, her father sends his henchmen, including the narrow-minded and villainous fiancé, to take her back home.

As Andi stepped carefully up the old worn wooden steps of the *Roxy Theatre*, slippery from the light drizzly rain. She tried to imagine how this place would have looked in its heyday. She could picture the bustle of theatre-goers all decked out in dresses, hats, beads and feathers. Perhaps girls were giggling coyly by the steps as young men stood around in their suits and hats looking suave and debonair. In the 1920's, there would be posters advertising new releases, the bold black and white prints hand painted in gaudy colours. Photos of Lillian Browning's sad lashes would greet theatre-goers in the foyer of red carpet with gold paisley swirls. Andi glanced at her flat court shoes, damp from the rain, standing on the threadbare carpet, worn down in patches to the brown hessian backing. This theatre had accommodated countless patrons in its time.

Andi tugged on Jo's reluctant hand. They went over to the little glass booth and slid their money through the circular hole. An uninterested attendant sat there in a white shirt, with silver bands above his elbows, a bowtie and vest. He mumbled and passed over their tickets. Even his boredom with the whole event could not dampen Andi's enthusiasm. The usher at the door was an older lady also dressed twenties style. She took their tickets and smiled in appreciation at Andi's outfit. "Oh darling... just *love* your beads," she gushed, in keeping with her character-role. "I got mine all the way from Parrie!"

Jo rolled her eyes melodramatically. "My dear, why *would* you go to all that trouble? Paris is *such* a long way away. My friend found her beads at Targhét!"

Andi laughed and blushed delightedly. "Thank you. I thought they did suit..." she said modestly, pinching Jo's arm to silence her sarcasm. She really could be there - in another era, in another life!

The lady chuckled and patted Andi on the hand amiably. "I just love a clever bargain hunter. I'm sure you will enjoy the movie," she said.

Andi and Jo walked into the dim corridor of the theatre. The musty smell of old drapes and rows of dusty leather theatre seats greeted them. The aisle had the same threadbare carpet, and the wooden floor under the seats was dark and stained from countless years of patrons spilling movie treats on the floor. The walls were hung in generous layers of gaudy red drapes. Swags regally framed the stage, moth holes and small rips in the lavish fabric telling of an age past. Peeling gold paint trimmed the yellowed wall above the screen. It was splashed with faded blue swirls that framed little painted country scenes. Flickering fake candles stood in a heavyset candelabrum that dimly lit the stage. She kind of wondered why the historical society hadn't tried to refurbish and renovate but had instead gone with the crusty worn look. Nothing chic about this shabbiness. Even soap and water might demolish this tenuous hold on the past.

"I want to sit right down the front," Andi whispered.

"Do we have to?" said Jo reluctantly.

"Yes, definitely. I want to feel as if we were really there! If I have to look at the collar of someone's grubby polo shirt all night, it will ruin the effect entirely."

Jo said nothing but sunk down low in the uncomfortable lumpy seats. She was hoping no one she knew would see her. This was by far the most embarrassing thing her best friend had asked of her in a long time.

She was relieved when the electric candles faded and

the organist took his seat. In the moment of quietness, they could hear rain on the roof and the low rumble of thunder.

Their hostess gave an introductory spiel that was short and to the point. The theatre was old. The black and white movie was silent, except for the live organ accompaniment. Generally, she told them, audiences of this era were not silent. 'Interactive' was not just a term coined for contemporary virtual computer games. "Hiss the villain; applaud the heroine!" she encouraged. A group of grannies behind them clapped loudly and cheered when she said that. Jo didn't dare turn around and check them out, although she really wanted too. Fancy getting this excited over a bit of nostalgia.

The organ wheezed out an opening cord. The reels spluttered light onto the screen and the credits started to roll. Date palms and rolling sand dunes framed the introductory caption: "The Persian province of Shiraz…"

The camera rolls towards an exotic eastern palace and another caption fills the screen. "A modern princess in a land rich with tradition…" Lillian Browning bursts into the palace garden dressed in a filmy Persian dancing costume, her dark hair fringed with feathers. Distressed, she turns to the older woman bedecked in jewels, who followed her. The scene blanked out and as the next caption framed with scrolls and swirls flashes up: "Mother,

I honour my father – the King. But I want an education before I marry!"

In spite of her vows to merely tolerate this primitive form of entertainment, Jo was soon quietly hissing the villainous fiancé and cheering the beautiful Princess Shahnaz. Along with Andi she followed the progress of this woman's breath-taking determination to surmount the odds stacked against her, in search of love and happiness. Fleetingly Jo mused that the ideas seemed quite modern for such an old film.

The black and white scenes continued to roll: there was the cowardly robbery; her job at the struggling dance-theatre; the bankers who threaten to close the theatre. Even the couple's romance was intermingled with captions that were like the punctuation in a sentence. A full screen shot was certainly not inconspicuous like a line of subtitles, yet they didn't seem to disrupt the flow of the story. Even the lack of colour blushing the heroine's cheeks did not distract. They became so absorbed that the black and white frames seemed to develop a natural hue of their own.

The Princess Shahnaz comes out of the theatre dressing rooms. Her face glows as she dreams of her handsome, but poor theatre proprietor-director, Antonio. She is dressed to learn a new dance, the Charleston – which is so different from her Persian repertoire. The organ growled a low menacing tremolo. Behind the curtain lurks the ugly henchmen poised to kidnap. But cleverly, she detects the slight flutter of fabric, and quickly flees. A chase ensues: across the stage, behind the curtains, around the backstage props. The organ player skips over the keys in allegro panic. The grannies in the audience go wild, cheering her on. Just then, Shahnaz sees Antonio tied to the stage scaffolding, but as her pursuers circle in, she is powerless to help her beloved. One villain slips and the organ music slides to the bass notes with a crash. More thunder added to the effect in stereo.

The organ resumes its hasty crescendos as Shahnaz takes advantage of the chaos and runs out onto the stage and back behind the curtains of the stage. Suddenly Shahnaz bursts from behind the curtains and runs down the centre aisle of the theatre. Breathlessly she stops beside Jo and desperately grabs her to her feet! She shakes her melodramatically by the shoulders. Andi jumps up, enthralled by the creative stage craft that would fashion the illusion of bringing the film to life. Shahnaz grabs her hand too and pulls them both out the side door and backstage. Someone is yelling, "Cut! Cut!" as Shahnaz runs to the dressing room and locks the door – reinforcing it with a chair under the knob.

"That'll buy us some time. Why did you take so

long?" whispered Shahnaz.

The girls stared at her in shock. Even Jo had to admit the effect of using live theatre during the film was quite exciting.

"He said you'd be there during the chase-scene. But this was our third take. I was running out of things I could muff. Never mind – you're here now." A knock at the door interrupted them. She swore and looked around in dismay. "I was not expecting you. I thought they would send someone much older. Good cover I suppose: the unexpected." She quickly checked the reinforced door and pushed a dresser in front of it.

She ran to a rack of clothes ripping off her wig of dark tresses as she went and stuffed it in a bag. Underneath the wig was smooth blonde twenties hair that looked exactly like the photos Andi had seen in the books from the library. It could have just been washed and blow-dried. Grabbing a few dresses and some shoes she flung them in the bag as well. "Here – take these," she said to Jo. "They'll be too big, but we haven't got time to change now. Bring them with you. Follow me."

She flew around the room quickly knocking things over and making a mess. She hurriedly grabbed a razor blade and unflinchingly cut her finger pad. The blood flowed freely as she allowed drops to fall on the carpet.

Then she opened the blacked-out windowpane and stuffed the gauzy curtain under the window sash, making sure blood was visible on the sill. Then in one final act of violence she smeared her hand on the mirror. When she grabbed a clean handkerchief to wrap up her finger and flung open the wardrobe.

Andi and Jo had not moved. Their mouths were gapping like plaster clowns in a side-show alley. The banging at the door was getting much louder.

"Come on!" she hissed as she climbed inside the wardrobe. "We can't wait any longer." She came back impatiently and pulled them in behind her.

* * *

2

They ran, almost scurried, bent over, along a damp, low tunnel. There was timber reinforcement along the walls and their only light was a hurricane lamp that swung wildly as they went. Weird shadows played havoc with their minds. Andi tripped on something and let out a terrified squeal. Jo clapped her hand over her mouth to suppress the noise. Even though she didn't know why, she certainly knew they needed to be quiet.

They were led around a couple of bends into a small room. It was more like an underground cave, dark and dingy. The lady put the lantern on the table and rubbed her hands on her dress. She seemed unconcerned at the sweaty smears that they left. Blood had started to seep through the bandage on her finger.

She closed a door and turned to the girls. "The previous theatre owners were Dutch or something - totally paranoid. They got very industrious during the war and made this bomb shelter. Ridiculous really – The War was never going to get this close to Australia. Still, it works for me. I've used it a number of times to exit when I need to escape overly enthusiastic fans and party-goers. I'm not sure if the authorities know about the tunnel, so we had better be quick. Where are they?"

Jo and Andi's pupils were dilated wide in the dim light and their faces extraordinarily pale. "Who?" they asked in unison.

"Not 'who'! My documents… from Mr Jones."

Jo and Andi looked at each other. "What documents?"

"The passport, birth certificate, bank books and tickets. I've paid for them…"

"We don't have them," said Andi honestly. "Look Princess Shahnaz, I think there's been a mix up…"

"Princess Shahnaz? You're kidding!"

"You're not Shahnaz?" asked Andi hesitantly.

"Of course, I'm Shahnaz but…" She sounded exasperated.

"We're not doing… well you know, live theatre?" asked Jo glancing around the walls for hidden cameras. There was no other explanation she could think of… a "reality TV" set up, or a spontaneous catch-you-out improvisation scenario. Perhaps they'd even get paid if they went along.

She looked at them stunned. "Of course, we're not doing theatre! The stage is back there. You don't see any cameras, do you? Don't tell me you are cast extra's! You were not there before… I memorized every face… I thought..." She stared at them and then sat down on the single wooden chair by the table and covered her face in her hands. "I don't believe it! Not after all this!"

Jo and Andi looked at her slumped shoulders. Suddenly she looked up and Andi saw that same sad, despondent glow in her eyes. "You're Lillian Browning," she said softly.

"Not anymore. I'm going to disappear..."

* * *

Harry Dunn walked wearily back to his tenement house. He looked up at the grey skyline and sighed just a little wistfully. Why did the city always seem claustrophobic? There was always something to clutter one's vision. Taking the tram down to the beach was the closest thing he had found to a place where he could look out at the sweeping horizon without interference. Some evenings, when the ache for home got a little too intense, he would take sandwiches and sit on the dunes. He'd watch the waves roll in hour after hour under the light of the moonrise.

He unlocked the door and went inside. Everything about this place grated on him. Especially the little things – like locking up his house. No one ever locked up at home. There was no need. Besides, how could the neighbours bring in your mail or feed the dog if you were inadvertently detained on some mercy mission.

Here, neighbours were strangers and so very suspicious, even Mr and Mrs Agostinelli next door. They used to give him generous amounts of tomatoes, onions and basil from their pocket-handkerchief garden. He could never eat the amount they thought one person required. He had tried to make conversation, but it was just an urban art that refused to sit comfortably on his lips. One day, with an arm full of tomatoes, he asked after the health of their daughter. After that they kept the dark eyed Sonia out of sight for fear of her virtue, and the tomatoes were suddenly attacked by a severe blight which meant there were none to spare. Harry decided trust was something that didn't come easily in the city.

Mostly it was easier for Harry to keep to himself, go to work, come home. Sunday was a relief. On Sunday, he could go to church. God never expected airs and graces. The people at church had become like the family Harry missed at home. Still, it wasn't the same.

He looked in disgust at the dull walls of his apartment and felt them closing in on him again. It was going to be another beach night tonight. He sawed off a few slabs of stale bread and slapped them together with some salted beef. He stuffed them in a paper bag, grabbed his keys and did an about turn. He felt like a fish out of water… or more like something that was drowning. He was getting so tired of paddling – constantly treading water. On evenings like tonight, he felt the water thrashing over his head. He wondered how long he could keep working so hard at something he knew would just never work.

The tram rattled and rocked. He stood up, hanging onto the rail even though there were spare seats so late in the evening. Even the confined space of a seat in the open carriage was too restricting. As the bell clanged, he swung off the standing board and walked briskly toward the restless sound of the waves. A family – late from an afternoon beach outing, the man in a dark suit, his wife trailing an umbrella and a little girl in a straw hat, saluted as they hurriedly passed to catch the last tram home.

Harry sat quietly and drank in the sensations of space. On these excursions he could almost have sworn he was in Church. It gave him that same feeling of the presence of God. Here he could pray. Here his thoughts were clearer.

He sat for ages and finally stirred himself to eat. He looked at his hands and realised in his haste he hadn't even washed off the grease from the work-shop. He rubbed them on his trousers and shrugged in a boyish disregard for honest dirt. He almost smiled as he thought how his Ma would react. She was a stickler about cleaning up for meals. In the end he went down to the water, scooped up a paw of wet sand and rubbed down his brown forearms, and rinsed off in the salty foam. Swimming in the surf never tempted him. A muddy dam, even a strong river current didn't faze him – but he figured swimming in agitated, turbulent surf would be like trying to sleep on a bed of nails: it ain't natural, it ain't fun, and it probably ain't healthy.

Harry settled back beside his brown paper lunch bag and glass water bottle, corked with a stopper. He washed the dry bread down with water that tasted like the tank needed a good flush from dead frogs and bird bits. A piece of beef fell from his bread, he picked it up and shredded it, tossing it to some tiny crabs that were flicking sand out of their holes in the low light of evening.

Later, when he thought about it, he would say it was the closest thing he ever experienced to hearing the voice of God. As clear and distinct as if his friend Jesus was sitting beside him on the dune, Harry heard Him say, or perhaps he felt him say – he wasn't exactly sure: *"You can go home now Harry. It's time."*

Harry paused, chewing his mouthful. One would never speak with your mouth full – especially to God. He carefully swallowed, "Really?" he responded.

"Yes," and a peace washed over him in waves like the sea rolling in on the sand before him. He was not a man given to emotion, but when he finally went to take another

bite of his sandwich, it tasted as salty as the ocean. He realised the tears that streamed down his face were of sheer relief… like he had been unconsciously holding his breath for six years and now he had suddenly been given air. "Thank you," he said, "Oh, thank you."

* * *

Lillian sat resigned, resting her head tiredly on the bare table. She waited for the heavy stomp of boots to echo along the hollow tunnel coming to take her away. She had one small suitcase and a small packed lunch in a handbag. "I was supposed to be eating this on the train… with my new life ahead of me." She looked at it in disgust and handed it to the girls. They politely declined.

"What's wrong with your present life?" Andi looked at her sitting there, the glamour and fringes of her dress looking oddly out of place in this bare underground room.

She shrugged tiredly. "It won't matter very soon…" she sighed.

Jo sat down on the floor and took a deep breath. She was seriously starting to suspect the actress was no longer acting. Tingles crawled up her spine.

"Lillian, why do you have to disappear?" asked Andi quietly, realising that Jo was not being very helpful. She must be in serious trouble if she needed a whole new identity.

Suddenly Lillian looked up. "Are you here to turn me in?"

Jo suppressed a low laugh. "Turn you in? To what? A frog for a prince to kiss? Don't you think that's a little out of our league?"

Lillian shook her head and pinched the bridge of her nose as if the pressure would somehow clear her head. The bungled plan totally messed with her equilibrium. Now she didn't know what to do. She couldn't go back. "The Feds have been investigating..." she said finally.

"Investigating what?" asked Andi confused.

"The Federal Police? They are investigating *you?*" asked Jo sitting up straighter. This string-bean actress looked too benign to be a serious threat to public security.

"They are on one of their witch-hunts," said Lillian.

"What did you do?" asked Andi.

"Do? You don't have to *do* anything!" said Lillian, the heat in her voice rising. "They investigate anyone – just for being successful... or for being popular... for just being!" She spat the words out in disgust. "I haven't even 'made it' yet... but we're expecting *The Daughter of Shiraz* to do well. I've fought so hard to get this role... and now my life is mush – my ambitions will never be realised. They've hounded me. I can't take it anymore!"

"Can they do that? What about invasion of privacy?"

"What about it? If they say it is a matter of national security, they can invade whatever they like."

"That doesn't sound very Australian, being 'the lucky country' and all!"

"Lucky?" scoffed Lillian in disgust. "The War-to-end-all-wars might be over, but there's a bigger invasion happening right under our noses. And no-one cares."

"Maybe they do care. Maybe that is why they look into things," offered Andi.

"They need someone to blame - that's all."

Jo shifted her weight restlessly as she sat on the floor. "You're suffering a conspiracy complex! I'm sure no one's out to get you," she said with just enough condescension to rile Lillian's ego.

"Don't give me 'conspiracy theory'!" she bit back harshly. "I wouldn't expect *kids* to understand the constant surveillance, the ears always listening, the questioning, the double-play by people I thought were my friends!"

Jo was seriously questioning the mental stability of this glamorous, yet totally paranoid, actress. "You *really* believe it – you *are* looking for a monster under every rock and a villain behind every lamp post! This is life, not a movie set."

Lillian stood up, restlessly fingering the ring on her hand. She glared at Jo through narrowed eyes. "It's *them* that are looking for a villain under every rock," she said, her grammar degenerating as the intensity in her voice rose. "That villain has a name: Communism - the Red Peril. That's it – pure and simple. The American industry is rife with propaganda and FBI witch-hunts. Australia is just taking a leaf out of their copybook... why they would bother I don't know. American politics are just dragging us down. Australian films are the cream! But our industry can't survive if they destroy every person with talent that comes along."

Jo laughed. "Australia – better than the Americans at making films. Yeah right!"

Lillian sat down again and looked at Jo with the disdain of one who is in the industry loop. "You have no idea," she said. Then she paused again. "You think I'm delusional. But I'm not. To start with I thought it was an obsessive fan stalking me. I'd see the same person outside the theatres after rehearsals or disappear around the corner near my unit. Everywhere I'd go – I'd see a glimpse of his hat and brown coat. A loony like that attacked a friend of mine. I hired a Private Investigator to trail him so I could get a restraining order."

"And..." both of them were listening intently now, regardless of their scepticism.

"The first investigator took my money and ran. The

second guy said something came up and he couldn't take the case. At least he refunded part of his fee." She paused. Andi got the impression it was more for dramatic effect than to clarify her thoughts. "Finally, I got hold of a man who came highly recommended, but charged like a wounded bull. His name was Mr Jones. He told me there was no fixated fan, just a very determined Federal investigator…"

Jo quietly sniggered. "Oh boy! What a scam. Fancy giving money to a guy who calls himself 'Mr Jones'!"

Lillian ignored her. "Jones said the Feds have a file on me that makes the collective works of Shakespeare look like a country gazette…"

"Yeah right." Jo could not restrain her interjection. This was definitely too farfetched. No wonder the lady was an actress – she had a jolly good imagination… and an ego to match.

"Sooner or later, I would be brought in for questioning about my 'communist sympathies'. I could be charged and put in gaol. That's when I agreed to leave sooner rather than later. I've done some rotten things, but…" her voice trailed off and she licked her lips as if something bitter was lingering in her mouth.

"So, are you?" asked Andi quietly.

"What?"

"A communist."

"That is the whole point – isn't it? Whether I am or not shouldn't be under investigation – or Australia isn't a free country. That was the whole reason behind The Great War. My brother died in that war. If you ask me - he died for nothing!"

"But they fought communists."

"No, actually they were fighting the fact we would *not* be given a choice. They happened to be communists, but they could have been anything… fascists, socialists, commercialists, imperialists…anything! It was so we could be free… and choose to hold to any creed or philosophy we want."

"But just for the record… are you?" Andi persisted.

"I'm not going to dignify that with an answer!"

* * *

The train pulled out of the station. Steam hissed and the wheels screeched, groaning as the carriages lurched forward. The girls sat in the deep leather bench-seats facing each other. Their few bags were stacked on the wrought iron racks above their heads. Lillian and the girls were the only ones in the carriage. It had a scribed sign above the window: "*Ladies*". The conductor had escorted them with a protective arm to the car set aside for ladies travelling alone without a chaperone. He assured them with a tobacco-stained smile that he would check on them frequently.

Lillian carefully looked down the station platform as the train clanged and rocked away. She slowly let out her breath. There was no sign of that coated man who had become her silent shadow. He was the reason she tolerated the girls hanging around. No one knew of them. If the investigator was trailing her, she didn't think he would be looking for three people travelling together. If Lillian had bothered to think about it, she would not have been able to account for why the girls came to still be here. She had made a mistake in a moment of panic and somehow, they stuck with her, like flies to fly-paper.

Andi and Jo reminded Lillian of her old school friend – Gladys. Together, they had been an inseparable twosome. Back then they were normal, honest girls who shared each other's highs and lows. But one day, Glad suddenly accused her of being self-absorbed in a scramble to get ahead. She told Lillian quite clearly what she thought, and Lillian had just turned and walked away. She didn't want to be stuck in the rut of mediocrity that characterised life in that small country town. She had lost Glad's friendship, but she didn't care. Not then.

She noticed that Jo and Andi had that same quality of candid honesty. In a desperate moment of extreme anxiety, it suggested to her mind that going back to the town she grew up in was the only way forward. In twelve years, she had gone home just once, nearly five years ago. That time she came and left in the dark. She had seen Glad on that brief visit under the cover of night and she swore then she would *never* go back.

That was before she had any way of knowing that all her sacrifices would come to nothing. She had to admit that the cost of fame and fortune had been high. Every day for years she told herself that living below the bread-line was the best diet a tuppence could buy… because it certainly didn't buy food! What luck that the willowy-thin-look is the latest fashion. She had enjoyed a status of relative comfort when she was doing concerts for soldiers going off to war. But when the concerts stopped so did the income.

After that she lived in a grimy flat and hocked everything that was of value to get by. She had pawned all her jewellery; except the ruby ring she had bought after she landed her first paying job. It had taken ages to pay it off. Even when things were at their lowest, she couldn't bring herself to part with it. Ever since she could remember, she had wanted a ruby ring. She always liked pretty things, and since her childhood was anything but pretty, she protectively hung onto this ring. She took on the vilest acting roles and kept the most unsavoury company – going to endless parties, just to be seen by directors and producers in the hope of being offered that role which would make her career.

She had auditioned for every part available in stage plays and musicals, but few parts were offered to her. Then she had landed the extraordinary opportunity of being cast in the most sought-after script in a new moving-picture with an excellent director. She was ecstatic – even though films were the sort of entertainment most serious actors knew would never amount to anything. Lillian was rather amused that her greatest strength – her singing voice, could not be featured in a silent moving picture, or "movie" as people were starting to call them. The popularity of these movies was surprising everyone. Lillian was now being offered leading roles. She had finally got to the place where she could achieve the kind of success she had always aspired to.

Just when the years of scraping and elbowing had finally started to pay-off, it was suddenly ripped out from underneath her. Mr Jones made it clear Lillian would never win this fight against the authorities. They had sabotaged her career. She tried to fight it to start with, but it seemed that a suffocating band was being drawn tighter and tighter around her throat. She looked out of the carriage at the passing ramshackle houses by the railway tracks and sighed. In the end she had also succumbed, and sunk onto the growing pile of anonymous 'Try-hards': those who were cast aside by the ruthless entertainment industry. In giving up, she admitted failure, and that knowledge bit into her soul like a pit-bull terrier. It wouldn't let go. She told herself it was better to get out and salvage the bits of her life that she could, but Lillian was not even sure that what was left was even worth salvaging.

The houses thinned out and the suburban sidings grew further apart. Lillian hardly moved. She sat by the window deep in her thoughts, mindlessly fingering the ring on her hand as she watched the world pass her by. Her fashionable felt hat with its broad-band and flat bow at the front, was pulled down, conveniently concealing her face. Her fair hair was sleek and smooth as always. Andi kept glancing at her, wondering what thoughts crowded her mind. Finally, she cleared her throat. "Lillian? Where are we going?" She barely stirred. Andi repeated the question.

"A little place called Gum Ridge. Murray's Siding is where we get off."

"Gum Ridge?" Jo laughed. "Never heard of it!"

Lillian didn't look offended. "I'm not surprised. That's why I left - twelve years ago… and that's why I'm going back. I told no one I came from there, so it should be a safe enough place to disappear."

"Twelve years is a long time… is your family excited

about you coming home?"

For the first time Lillian's face showed a flicker of emotion, but she quickly smoothed the lines. She knew she could cleverly act out the part of the repentant prodigal – but she had no intention of living a lie – not anymore. They could take her or leave her, the way they found her. Instinctively she guessed how they would respond. "They will be shocked… maybe angry. They don't know I'm coming… because of the phone taps I couldn't risk it. Besides it won't give them the chance to say no."

"Aren't you worried?"

Lillian was unmoved, her face like flint. "I have no choice," she said, and then turned and looked out the window again.

But Jo didn't want to sit in sombre silence anymore. The monotonous rocking and chugging of the train, interspersed with the occasional steam blown whistle quickly lost its sense of novelty. "Tell us about this Gum-place. What do people do there?"

"People at Gum Ridge do what people do everywhere. Eat, work, sleep, and get up again." Lillian just wanted to be left alone with her self-reflective depressing thoughts.

"What do they do for fun?" asked Jo. It sounded like a grave-yard would be more entertaining.

"Not much."

"Well, what work do they do?"

"Look," said Lillian suddenly. "It's a dump of a place. I hated being there and that is why I left. It's got a school, a post-office that's also a general store; there's a pub, a community hall, a few shops, and a church. The houses are little and the farms are dull. My father was killed in a fire when I was eight. My brother and I lived with my Grandparents after that, just until my mother got herself back together. Except she never did. That's it. The sum total of Gum Ridge. Not exciting at all."

"Why not go somewhere else then?"

"There is nowhere else."

"Sure, there is. There was a whole planet – last time I checked."

"Yeah well. My planet just shrunk to the size of a corner-shop and a pub."

* * *

3

Harry sat on the back steps beside the old Kurrajong tree that grew near the small farmhouse. Brilliant diamond-stars studded across the black velvet sky. On a night like tonight, he would have normally grabbed his traps and gone after some rabbits. He took a deep breath and sighed. That sigh should have been the overflow of contentment from a long-awaited homecoming. It was in a way, but the state of the farm shocked him.

His father and mother had struggled. Harry was saddened by how aged they looked. They were tired and worn out – simple as that. The regular payment that Harry sent home from the city was to keep them in comfort, but in an attempt to try and fix things they often went without even basics and poured the money into the farm like water onto sand. It just disappeared.

Moths played in the light from the kerosene lantern hanging on the back porch. It threw thin streaks of light out over the house yard. The yard was small and bare, uncreative with a few spindly geraniums and some self-sown zinnias and Ma's struggling vege patch. But it was what was beyond the picket fence that held his gaze. He stared at the grotesque silhouettes that grew like deformed monsters marauding his land. Everywhere he looked cactus crowded his vision: the cursed Prickly Pear.

When he left six years ago it was a problem they had struggled with for years. It made the land unusable. It choked out their crops and the pasture. It even grew down the centre of the dirt cart tracks, and crawled up into the branches of trees. Not an inch of space was exempt from this invading tyrant.

They had to get rid of all but a few of head of stock and the house cow, because they couldn't feed them. The animals couldn't eat the prickly-pear straight out of the paddock. The fine bristles stuck in the soft skin of their mouths, causing such severe irritation they were unable to eat anything until they were weak bags of bone. It was a constant job of feeding them by hand, and the irony was that the only thing available to feed them was… more prickly-pear. Every day Harry's father chopped down cactus and using a hay pitch fork seared the fine bristles off piece by piece over an open fire, just like making toast on a camp-fire. At least it kept them alive. The house cow went all but dry, and what little milk she did give, had a bitter cactus taint to it. His Pa constantly reminded them that they were one of the lucky ones. At least they still had animals and a farm to keep them on.

Together, he and his father had tried every strategy

they could think of to control the pest-pear. They would cut it back and try to burn it. But cactus is green and doesn't burn well. They suffered cuts and gashes to their arms and faces and had to endure painful nights when the fine prickly hairs stuck through their shirts and could not be seen to pick out. Eventually they festered like a shingles rash, and the blisters and weeping sores would give them agonizing nights, restless without relief.

They ploughed the pest in, but no sooner was the soil turned, then it would come back with a vengeance – more determined and more virulent than ever. They tried every tactic the locals could think of. They had public meetings in the community hall and collaborated... pooling their ignorance and supporting each other through the crisis.

Out of these meetings they concocted lethal recipes for chemical cocktails of arsenic and caustic soda. Then the neighbours would get together in large spraying gangs to try and get it under control. They even tried the ideas of pen-pushing academics in the city. One of those strategies was to drive a big clumsy boiler on a metal cart through large areas of pear. Another idea was to fumigate the pest by boiling a solution of arsenic in the vat and vaporising toxic clouds of poison over the stands of pear. The operators got sick but the pear kept on growing. Every line of attack, every attempt they tried, made no lasting impact.

Gradually the neighbours had given up and left, deserting their homes and farms in desperation, one by one. That's when Harry left too. He couldn't bear the thought that his parents would have to go. He figured it would kill them. So, he went to the city and found a job in a foundry – applying his trade as a blacksmith. He sent all but a meagre allowance for himself back home. The work was repetitive and tedious. When his shifts allowed, he worked a second job for a motorcar garage. The pay was little to start with, but he was fascinated with this new horseless technology. He figured he was entitled to some 'play-time'. It also kept his mind from rusting out of boredom.

He started in the garage doing rouse-about jobs. He kept his eyes and ears open and read any information he could get hold of. He quickly learnt the workings of engines and carriages. His boss gave him more and more responsibility, and he gradually acquired his own tools of the trade. It was not long before they put him on full-time with full-pay and he was able to leave the factory. Oh, happy day that was! He could see so much potential for custom-made farm machines – if there ever came a time where useable farmlands appeared again.

With the money he sent home, his parents had bought up one of the neighbouring blocks in Harry's name. Basically, they wanted to help out their neighbours, since they had a young family and their plight seemed more serious than their own. That block ran right down to the main road near the town, but as Harry silently looked at the clusters of spreading pear that choked the life out of the land, he wondered how wise that decision was. Perhaps they should have kept the money to try and keep themselves afloat. Some called the pear 'the giant green octopus'. He never saw anything in the ocean that compared to this monster. It was why the town was dying. He wondered if God had sent him home so he could offer up his last respects and witness the funeral.

Harry hadn't told his parents of his experience by the sea that inspired him to come home. They would most certainly think the fumes of the Big Smoke had affected his brain. They were torn between the delight of having him home, and the burden of worry that the threat of going-under placed on them. They couldn't understand why he had suddenly quit a stable job and turned up.

Harry knew his Ma worried he had 'girl-trouble', but nothing could have been further from the truth. There had been no girls, not for a long time. When he was a boy, his heart had been stolen by a blond-haired beauty who had dumped him in search of fame and fortune. He knew that he had been just a kid and it should not have meant anything; but it had, and for now, girls didn't interest him.

Besides, city-girls were a breed apart and all the evidence agreed with him.

He looked up at the clear night sky and reminded himself again that the Voice of God had said it was "*time*". He knew it was God. That was something Harry was very sure of. With determination, Harry set his jaw and although there was no evidence of anything *being* okay, he turned-in for the night. He rested on his bed, solid in the belief that God doesn't make mistakes. He's not a mean god who would say something deliberately ambiguous – just for the sake of it. If God had said it was time, then His timing was perfect. "If what I am looking at is not okay – it must be soon. Real soon," he whispered in faith, as he turned down the lamp-wick and went to sleep.

* * *

A boy and his mother joined the girls in the unescorted "Ladies" carriage. As soon as the woman had sat down, she immediately began to bemoan the heat and the cold and the wet and the dry; the hard seats and the long days and every other affliction that makes a traveller's lot miserable. The boy had sat picking his nose and swinging his boots hard against Andi's legs. She moved over and he tenaciously followed her in an uncompromising quest for a clout under the ear. Andi glared pointedly at the woman, who took that look to mean she was fascinated by her monotone conversation. Andi became the victim of an ear bashing by the mother and a leg bashing by the kid.

The conductor walked through the carriage, the noise of the train getting louder as the door opened and then slammed behind him as he called out, straining his husky smoker's voice, "Murray's Siding… Murray's Siding for Gum Ridge – next stop." It was the sweetest sound ever!

The girls quickly dragged their bags off the luggage racks and struggled around the boy's legs as he dangled them obstinately in the way. Jo caught him poking out his tongue as they turned away and she suddenly found her near empty bag extremely heavy. She pushed her bag so it squeezed his legs firmly back into place. "Conductors have a special box in the luggage car for rude little boys," she hissed under her breath as she bent down to adjust the straps on her case. "So, watch your manners." Jo looked up at his mother with a glowing smile. "Enjoy the rest of your trip Ma'am," she said and then followed the smoking haze of the conductor to the door.

There was no platform, so they waited as he manoeuvred the portable steps into position. They stepped down onto the gravel beside the tracks. The siding was deserted except for the conductor and guard who quickly got back on the train. He waved his flag and the train hissed once more, billowing black bitter coal smoke as it strained and chugged up the line. The train disappeared around a bend, blasting a funnel of steam through its whistle as it approached a crossing.

The siding seemed very lonely in the early morning mist. Lillian turned to the girls. "We'll get a room at the hotel. It's around the corner opposite the post-office. Don't expect an open arm reception."

"Why?" Her verdict was such a foregone conclusion that Jo figured it probably involved more than failing to send Christmas cards.

"Things change that's all. Oh. One more thing: I'm not Lillian Browning here. My name is Daisy. Daisy Brown. Lillian has never existed. And if I find out you have said something…" A murderous look came into her eyes, and for the first time, Andi felt heebie-jeebies tickle up and down the back of her collar. Andi realised then that during her whole journey – even way back in the theatre, she had forgotten to pray. She never left her friend Jesus out of anything. Why would she not talk to Him when he landed her in an adventure of this scale? Oh, she needed help! Andi didn't want to exclude Him. She couldn't afford to.

"Just Daisy Brown?" echoed Jo. Where she imagined Andi would be tragically disappointed in a name that sounded so plain, so uninteresting… so unadventurous, Jo found it a relief… almost amusing. My, what one finds underneath the layers of pretence! It fitted her better in a way.

"Daisy Ann Brown is my birth name," she said as if she took particular delight in bursting the glamourous actress bubble.

Andi looked around at this plain railway siding with the weeds growing alongside the flat spongy leaves and yellow flowers of prickly pear. There was so much pear! They had potted some cactus to decorate their school hall for a Mexican theme social night one weekend. They had painted the tops of the terracotta pots in orange and blue zigzags. It had looked very Mexican and rather exotic then, but here the cactus just made everything take on a suffocating plainness. Even 'Lillian Browning' – the face that could captivate theatre audiences around the nation, without make-up seemed lacklustre and ordinary. Why, the heroine was supposed to be a bold, daring beauty who battled the odds… and won! Lillian's story was supposed to be like Princess Shahnaz played out in real life. *'Well, if this is real life, who wants it?'* thought Andi with disappointment. *"Lillian Browning's hometown is a dreary, lifeless, boring dump, just like she said… and it seems Daisy Brown's real life, is equally dull."*

Lillian picked up a light leather case, turned on her heel and walked across the tracks and up the road towards the post-office. The girls grabbed their things and followed after her in a hurry.

* * *

The proprietor of the hotel said little when Lillian asked for their rooms. He unhurriedly placed the keys on the counter next to Lillian's money. He sl-ow-ly counted it out and carefully tucked away the notes. Then he opened the register to the right page and meticulously spat on the end of a pencil. It wasn't only business that was slow in this town. "What name miss?" he asked with sluggish disinterest.

Lillian picked up the keys to their rooms. "Miss Daisy Brown," she said without missing a beat. The man froze – his pencil suspended halfway to the page.

"Dai...sy Brow...?" He seemed to gag on her name. His eyes narrowed as he stared at her face.

"Yes, that is correct. Daisy – that would be D A I S Y, like the flower. Brown – as in the colour, no E."

Even Andi could acknowledge that even though Lillian had not actually said anything rude, her voice was prickly and goading the man into a reaction. And sure enough, she had pressed some buttons. The man came to life and glared at her across the counter. "Don't get smart with me. I know who you are. We ain't got any lodg..."

"You've taken my money so I've paid for our rooms,

and I have the keys," Lillian interrupted. "We will be staying until I can find another residence. Which will *not* be very long I can assure you." She nodded then, more out of habit than courtesy and made her way toward the stairs. The man gapped after her as if he had seen a ghost.

The girls were in a twin room next to Lillian's. It was small and the walls were tarnished in dark brown shellac. There was an adjoining doorway near the washstand that had a chipped, plain basin and jug sitting on the top. The iron beds were small and sagged in the middle. Two narrow French doors opened onto a shallow balcony that overlooked the street. They sat out there for quite a while watching the small community slowly stir into its day, while they ate the last of the stale sandwiches that Lillian… no – Daisy, had given them. It was a most unsatisfactory breakfast, but they had nothing else. Andi glanced at Jo. "How is this going to work?"

Jo coughed on a dry crust and washed it down with water. "What do you mean?"

"Well, Lillian is *obviously* delighted about us being here: *not*! It was a mistake to stay with her. She's not going to want to keep paying our way."

Jo took another long drink of water. She felt dehydrated from train trip. She didn't want to worry about details like Andi did. If it wasn't for the pathetic evidence

45

of their breakfast that stuck in her throat, she probably would have dismissed their plight altogether. "I don't know," Jo said with a shrug. "I *do* know I've never seen anyone with such a big chip on their shoulder. It's the size of Uluru."

They fell into silence and watched a rather plain looking woman vigorously sweep the step of the post-office on the opposite side of the street. She kept staring up at them. Voices filtered through from Lillian's… no… Daisy's room. They couldn't get used to calling her just *Daisy*. It was a deep man's voice: "You've got a nerve coming back here now. You've no right after all this time!" There was a tremor in the voice, whether from age or tension, the girls could not tell.

"I have every right Sidney! It is a free country!"

"Well, ain't that rich! You've done your gallivanting around in the high life. That was your choice, and you made it. But you *have* no right now just to waltz back here and ruin our lives!"

"Gee whiz," whispered Jo on the balcony, "that was quick – we haven't even unpacked yet!"

"She said there wouldn't be any royal reunions – but I guess I didn't expect she'd be greeted with a hit squad!" said Andi quietly, turning her head on the side to hear what was being said.

Her voice was on edge. "Why not? I just want to see her," Lillian demanded, almost in a whisper.

"Daisy – you can't expect it! I won't have it…" And the clarity of their conversation faded as the voices became strained and angry. Steps, a door slammed and then silence. Deafening silence. Suddenly something crashed and then sobbing, muffled and heartrending.

The girls sat frozen staring out over the street, stunned. A tall, angular man with slicked-over, thinning hair appeared from under the awning of the balcony where they sat. He shuffled across the dusty street to the post office. He wore a white shirt with the sleeves rolled up to the elbows and a vest. The young woman who swept the post-office step with such fervour, met him at the door. She discarded her straw-broom and flung herself at him in a hard embrace. He guided her inside and through the glass door that stood slightly ajar, they could dimly see him awkwardly patting her shoulder in consolation.

Just then a tabby cat escaped through the front door, chased by a little girl with fair curls, in a frilled calico-dress. She sat on the step for a few minutes and carefully stroked its grey coat and then picked it up under the front legs and carried it breathlessly back inside.

When the girls thought the sobbing through the wall had subsided sufficiently, they gently knocked and opened the door that adjoined their rooms. She was lying across the bed; her eyes red and her shoulders still shuddered at random. The ceramic pitcher lay shattered on the floor by the door that led into the corridor. Lillian sat up irritably and dabbed her eyes. "You are like bush flies that hang around a horse's rear end. Why don't you get lost?"

Andi was taken aback. Her rudeness was not at all what she expected from a cultured, star-studded actress. She carefully retreated, but as she stepped back, she suddenly realised Lillian wasn't an actress – *that* was her job. She was just a person who was hurting, and if she wanted to be known as Daisy – so be it.

Andi looked at Daisy's red, swollen eyes too. *"God,"* she prayed silently, *"Do we leave? What's the best thing to do here?"* No instructions fell from the sky, so Andi stayed put.

"Well? What are you waiting for? I've got enough problems!"

Andi cleared her throat. Seeing Daisy as a person who was struggling gave her courage. "We know that this is not a good time…"

"You can bet your life on that! Go away!"

"…. However," Andi ignored her outburst. "We came with you to Gum Ridge because you seemed to think that it would help you get here unnoticed."

"Yeah well, I'm here now – so you can go."

"But we have no money and nowhere to go even if we wanted to. You paid for our tickets… remember?"

Daisy stared at them through red-rimmed eyes. "Send a telegram to your parents or something!"

Jo shook her head. "We can't. We're stuck here. We wanted to talk about what to do."

Wearily Daisy wiped her eyes with her palms in a resigned way. Nothing was ever simple: it was just one problem on another problem. It was so unfair! She had come back to Gum Ridge to salvage her life… but she could tell no one was going to let her. She'd been in town hardly two hours and it was like huge walls blocked her every turn. It was not even like she was asking for help. If they just left her alone – she'd be fine! Daisy stood up and poured a drink of water from a small jug on the shelf. She held the plain tumbler out of habit like a delicate cocktail glass. She rubbed the rim distractedly with the long finger that flashed her ruby ring in the light. She had looked out for number one for so long, it was beyond her selfish, spoilt experience to think about another person's position. "You've got *no* money?" she said quietly.

The girls shook their heads.

"No parents?" They confirmed it.

"Nothing?"

"We have these clothes…"

Daisy swore in an uncultured vent of every uncouth adjective she had ever heard. She waved her glass in frustration and threw it against the door to join the shattered pitcher, and then threw herself down hard on the bed. It creaked ominously, and slowly collapsed in on itself. The mattress and bed cover enveloped her gradually like she had been pushed down into a bowl of batter. The shock stunned her words into silence.

Jo and Andi were rendered momentarily speechless. Andi gasped in horror as Daisy sprawled like a doll thrown in a heap, her long legs sticking straight out – undignified and ungainly.

Unexpectedly Jo giggled. She covered her mouth in shock and muffled the laughter that refused to stay politely inconspicuous. Eventually she gave up and laughed outright. Andi stared, reproving her insensitivity, but then the contagion effect overwhelmed her and she smiled, not so much *at* Daisy, but over the whole thing… the string of events that saw them here at Gum Ridge.

First, their mistaken identity – how could they be seriously taken for undercover agents for a private investigator? Or the Federal Police? It was too much! Then there were the unbearable travel companions that made one think that being locked up in cage full of rabid dogs would be a preferable form of torture. Or the pub-owner who obviously had alerted all of Gum Ridge within seconds of their arrival. All this, and they just ended up in Gum Ridge. It was seriously back-blocks, and it seemed the people in this "hick" country town were totally oblivious to the limitations of this place.

To top it off, the collapsing bunk put Miss-high-and-mighty well and truly in her place! Daisy sat there glaring at them, trying to reclaim some sense of decorum. All she probably wanted to do was strangle someone – specifically them… and she was rendered helpless by a snare of bed sheets and pillows.

Sometimes a thing happens that is like a valve being let off a pressure cooker. What is normally un-funny suddenly seems incredibly hilarious. Jo slowly took a deep breath and looked at the expression on Daisy's face with her mussed-up hair that was usually immaculately sculptured, and helplessly started laughing again. They held their sides and hooted again when Daisy frowned in disgust and tried unsuccessfully to pull herself out of her trap of bedframe and blankets, sheets and pillows.

Slowly Daisy's face softened as she looked at these girls – homeless and completely dependent on her as the only apparent adult in their life. Yet they were not weighed down by failure or worry. Oh, to be young again… when life is uncomplicated and ambitions are fresh, and when laughter comes as easily as seeing the funny side of a disaster. She almost smiled as she unexpectedly realised her ridiculous predicament. Throwing herself back she abandoned herself and laughed until tears streamed down her face and she was gasping for breath and her sides hurt. It felt better than a gin and tonic.

The girls struggled to help her up, but the comical bubbles of laughter made progress impossible and only served to exaggerate the pickle she was in. Slowly their hilarity subsided and Daisy lay trapped in her bed-prison. She reached out and the girls hoisted her to freedom. Daisy stood, embarrassed in the silence, and momentarily gave each girl a hug, and then abruptly busied herself reconstructing the bed. Daisy recognised that this was the only time in twelve years she had laughed without the aid of a very strong cocktail-drink. Now she wondered, for the first time since coming back to Gum Ridge, at the possibility that somehow it might be okay.

* * *

4

The next day, after a breakfast of porridge, bread, and prickly pear jam, Harry quietly announced he was going to walk the boundary fence. He took his little testament bible and shoved it in his pocket. He loaded the horse with wire and supplies, a long-handled knife, a water bag, and swag, and shoved his rifle in the long leather pouch that hung from the saddle. He threaded and tied on a leather breast plate that he slung around the horse's neck and secured the leather leggings that ran down the horses' front legs that tied under the fetlocks. This protective armour allowed the horse to walk through the pear. They matched his own heavy leather chaps that had become something of standard dress whenever he went into the paddocks. He hadn't resorted to some local versions of using hammered out kerosene tins. That just seemed a little too Ned Kelly for him.

He set out with no real idea of how long he would be gone. He just needed to walk around the space that was his heritage… and his future. Most farms around here were about 600 acres: part of the government's post war selection scheme. Even in good times the "closer settlement blocks" were barely enough to support their owners. Theirs was a fair bit bigger than that, his parents were here long before the war. And then there was the neighbour's place they had bought up, which was there before the post war settlement project as well. Harry's ownership of that other farm didn't mean much to him. He couldn't see how they would ever support more than their own square bit of dirt; much less expect it could support them. If it was just there, he hoped it wouldn't be too great a burden.

He wound his way around the spreading clumps of cactus leading his horse, always following the line of the fence. Every familiar landmark seemed to be swallowed by the masses of dark green sponge. Bright yellow flowers and red fruit sat like jewels on top of their flat freckled leaves. He almost expected that sunlight would cause it to flash deep red like a facetted ruby. He grimaced. There was nothing precious about this plague. Harry hated the irony that the pest had been introduced to kick start a cochineal industry since the cochineal bugs loved the cactus. The ruby coloured dye was prestigious enough for the English to try and outwit the Spanish bid to corner a monopoly on the market. But the red dye industry that they hoped for never flourished, and the cactus went berserk. He stopped and hacked back large chunks of cactus with the long-handled knife so he could repair a section of fence where rabbits, 'roos and emus caused damage. Was he always cleaning up the mess of other people's misguided ambitions?

He worked wordlessly, mulling over everything his eyes saw and his mind tried to deny. Even with his mind so busy, his eyes constantly darted like scanners, always watching for a shape or a movement on the ground. His trained eye saw the curled round fat body of a death adder disguised in amongst the cactus, brown dirt and leaves. It was half buried in the loose soil, its thick diamond-head pointing silently out.

The death adder was an enigma to Harry. Every other snake he knew would try to escape unless it was threatened and cornered. This snake just lay still, waiting. Because of that, some people called them "deaf adders", in the belief they couldn't hear or detect sound when one came near. Harry figured its fat sluggish body could best make a strike by just letting their prey come close. He even watched one lure a small lizard within reach by wriggling his tail like a tantalizing grub. They were so common around the pear that an odd bush tale had emerged that the pear itself gave birth to the adder when it got to a certain size.

Harry's thick leather boots and long leather chaps had saved his life numerous times when he had accidentally stepped on these unseen death traps. Some in the district had not been so fortunate. It was just another dimension of the curse. The extent of destruction and death seemed to know no limit. Harry reached for his gun and there was one less adder in the plague. He looked grimly at the dead snake lying at the base of the sprawling prickly pear. If only the cactus-pest was as easy to remedy.

He went back to the fence. He watched some wispy emu feathers caught in the wire sway in the slightest puff of a breeze. Harry sighed. The emus were another problem. They relished eating the ripe red fig-sized fruit and the seeds were spread in their droppings as far as an emu could run. And emus can run. The government had even issued a bounty on emu eggs and heads... and crows.... and magpies. In an economy where nothing else brought a quick buck, the numbers of birds were fast being brought under control. But did it make any difference to the prickly-pear? *Time will tell,* was what his Pa had philosophically said about this and other government initiatives. If time was what they were waiting for... it didn't seem to make any difference at all.

Finally, he stopped and pulled his rabbit-felt hat from his head. "God," he said, "You know this land can no more support us all now than it could six years ago. I'm not saying I heard You wrong about coming back, but I need your wisdom to know what to do from here. You know we don't have the income from my city job to see us through. I've got a lot of time ahead of me Lord as I work the boundary, and I'm not given to chattiness. Would really appreciate you giving me ears to hear what to do."

It was probably the longest prayer that Harry had ever prayed in his life – except for the time when he wanted a puppy as a boy. He firmly replaced his hat and picked up the fencing pliers that lay by his boots. He went back to work in the companionable silence of one who is in the presence of a very good friend and words are unnecessary embellishments. He stopped only to have a smoko of bread and that eternal supply of prickly-pear jam before he resumed the trek further along the boundary.

* * *

"Well, there's nothing for it, except for us to look for a job," said Andi determinedly.

"I can't begin to imagine what," said Daisy pessimistically.

"But since so many people have left the district, there must be something left to be done," offered Jo. She pointed towards the post office. "What about postal deliveries?"

Daisy suddenly turned irritable. "What is it with the post-office? Every suggestion starts with the blessed post-office!"

"Well, it's all we can see from the balcony. There isn't much else in town," said Andi who thought that calling Gum Ridge a "town" was a gross exaggeration. But regardless of its isolation and lack of anything civilised, Andi was resigning herself to the idea of getting to know the personalities who would want to call this place "home".

But it wasn't boredom that kept Jo glancing at the post-office-shop. She was mesmerised by the little girl with light bouncy curls who would skip around on the sidewalk before the broom-lady would come and scoop her back inside. At other times the little girl would try to hoola-hoop, or scratch a hop-scotch game in the dirt, or dance with her cloth doll with red wool hair who was always her faithful companion. She'd wave at the ladies in sulkies as they drove past, or sometimes a motor-car would roar and splutter its way by and she would press her little nose up against the glass at the front of the shop, captivated by its noisy progress. Occasionally Jo caught Daisy looking at the little post-office-girl with the queerest look, but she always quickly turned away and busied herself with something quite unimportant as if it was of the highest priority.

"I thought the post-office should be as good a place to start as any," said Andi. "We don't have that many choices."

"I'll try anywhere else first. I doubt any of 'em will want to hire though," said Daisy as she went out the door.

* * *

Harry sat out under the stars and stared at the flames

of his small campfire. This was the last leg of the fencing perimeter. Tomorrow, if there were not too many more repairs, he'd be back at the house. Tonight. Surely tonight God would tell him his next move. He pulled out his testament and flicked opened the worn corners of the pages tilting them towards the flames to read the words. "If any of you lack wisdom, let him ask of God, that giveth to all men liberally..." He didn't think it necessary to actually ask – again, since God heard him the first time. He just read it once more and waited, patiently... like a child, scrubbed and presentable, sitting at the table knowing his mother was going to bring out a meal when it was ready. Harry's Ma always said, "The food is my job Son. You just do your bit to be ready." Harry had done his bit. He was waiting now for God to bring what he needed. His Ma never failed. Why would God do less? It never occurred to Harry that most kids would be squirming and wriggling and whinging and impatient. That was not his way. God's 'good time' was perfect. He would never leave him short. In actual fact, it said "*liberally.*"

Harry closed his eyes and took a deep breath. Being home was like waking up from a really bad dream. He listened to the sounds of the bush, and his horse hobbled nearby and inhaled the wood smoke and the smell of the earth. These smells were so different from the salt spray of the sea; the dry urban pavements heaped with rubbish and trash cans on collection day along dusty city streets. He conceded he didn't mind the puttering of engine fumes, the fuel and the grease at the garage where he worked. The garage was okay... and if he was honest – he was missing that.

Bang!

Harry opened his eyes wide. It was as sudden as if he had been shot with a gun. The idea was so foreign: so new, he realized it wasn't his. He also liked it – which made it kind of appealing. Open up a garage and workshop, here in Gum Ridge, along the main road so that travellers could stop and buy cans of fuel and get whatever repairs they needed, on their way to the city. And then there could also be a growing number of local motorists who were exploring the idea of motorised transport.

* * *

"Are you ready?" asked Jo as they braced themselves to go job-hunting. They had gone through Daisy's clothes and were dressed ready to launch themselves on Gum Ridge. Andi's eyes told the whole story. She didn't even have an out of school job at the local take-away shop where a lot of her friends worked. How would she ever seem credible here? Jo nodded. She understood. "Me neither. Let's go anyway."

They walked down the stairs and felt the icy judgment of the man behind the bar. They deliberately avoided eye contact and went out into the glaring sun. They stepped over the gutter and around the horse manure on the street, towards the post-office. The country-town street suddenly seemed as wide as the Nullarbor Plain. Daisy's pessimism definitely seemed more like a healthy dose of realism now. No one would hire, and they knew it before they even asked.

Andi squared her shoulders and lifted her chin. "Walk confident, think confident, am confident..." she muttered to herself as she opened the door and it jangled a clanging little bell.

"Good morning sir," she said cheerily to the thin man by the newspaper stand. His balding hair was swept over the top in thin greasy streaks. He wore the same vest they saw the other day as he left the hotel. His wardrobe evidently only consisted of white shirts that today had silver bands worn above his elbows that hitched up the length of the sleeve like metallic garters. The girls could see that up close there were grimy stains around the collar. The man's face was pock-marked from the scars of adolescent acne, and he had a Charlie Chaplain style moustache – or perhaps it was more like Hitler's. His small eyes were framed by thin wire rimmed glasses. The over-all effect was entirely intimidating. He looked at them grimly and said nothing.

"Hmm." Andi cleared her throat, trying to salvage her fast-fading courage. "Well, sir – we were wondering if you had any positions available. We are looking for work."

He stared at them through narrowed eyes, they were intense, magnified through the lenses. He abruptly turned away. "We have nothing."

"Just now or could we come back again later? Do you know who else we might ask?"

"No."

A mass of fair curls appeared at the door that led to the back of the living area behind the shop. The little girl tilted her head around the doorjamb and waved a shy sort of gesture at Jo who grinned at her, and whispered "Hello".

The man flung around violently, "Ruby! Go back to your mother. Now!" and he closed the door in Ruby's face. He turned back to them abruptly. "Is there anything you want to purchase?" he said curtly, his face flushing red.

"No – we don't have money because we don't have a job," said Jo rather smartly. She wasn't hurting anybody… particularly Ruby. He had no right to be so rude.

"Then you had best leave. Loiterers are not welcome," he said tersely.

"Loiterers?" sputtered Jo as they left the shop to the sound of the tinny little bell. "Loiterers! We were asking for honest exchange of labour for money!"

Andi looked up and down the street. There were a few other buildings. "Where now?"

Jo grimaced. This was so incredibly pointless. She forced herself to put a light lilt in her voice. "Well, in the words of a famous Austrian governess, 'Let's start at the very beginning – it's a very good place to start!'

"Really?" said Andi in despair. "Oh Jo, Maria Von Trapp is a long way from Gum Ridge!' She sighed. "Well, I guess they can only say 'no'," she said trying to reassure herself.

But 'no' was not the only thing they could, or did, say. People refused to let them in, one assistant yelled at them: "Get out! And don't show your faces in here again!" Another portly matron bellowed that the wrath of God and all the residents of Gum Ridge district was upon them. Everywhere they were confronted by irate, aggressive stares.

By the time they headed back to the hotel they were close to tears. They felt like beaten dogs, cowering away with their tails tucked tightly between their legs.

"You know what it is?" said Jo suddenly, "We're strangers."

"What happened to good old country hospitality?" said Andi.

"Well, you know – cliquey little communities don't

want the big, bad world invading the safety of their small, little lives. We represent progress – the outside. They're scared of us," said Jo sullenly.

Andi looked at her reflection in a shop window. "Truth be known... I'm scared of *them*. We can't even leave – we have no money! From what Daisy said, she hasn't got enough to pay our way... which I sincerely believe she would, just to get rid of us."

"Andi, apart from being stuck in a time-warp, we've been thrown into a vindictive, horrible dump of a place – with no one to look out for us!"

"We've got each other... and God. He's still looking out for us. I'm sure of it."

"Well, it doesn't feel like it – that's for sure," said Jo as they finally trudged up the stairs of the Hotel. They met Daisy coming down, holding her little leather suitcase that was secured with a strap around the middle.

"Where are you going?" they demanded as she pushed passed. They twirled on the stairs and followed her back out into the sunshine. She barely grunted at them, but walked along the sidewalk, passed the few shop fronts until the shade-awnings disappeared.

Daisy kept walking as if a break in pace would tip the world off its axis and cause some fatal interruption in the rhythm of the seasons. She crossed a street, barely pausing for a horse and sulky to go past. Eventually she stopped at the last visible house on the edge of town. It was a run-down little cottage that had lattice dangling precariously from the verandah. It boasted a lush lawn of prickly pear that was even climbing out over the sadly neglected yard-fence. The windows were boarded shut in a token effort to keep trespassers out.

Finally, Daisy turned, as if registering with great effort that the girls were beside her. "I have found a place to live," she said with dignity. She could have been standing on the threshold of Windsor Castle.

Jo spluttered as Daisy walked up to the verandah. Palings ripped from the fence were nailed across the front door, barring entry. "Are you *sure* this is suitable for human habitation?"

"It's got to be. It is rent free, until I can get a job..."

Andi was amazed. "You're kidding! We have a house for free?"

"Umm...well I made an arrangement because it is vacant. Having tenants will actually increase its value," she qualified carefully. "So, it's not really 'free'," she confessed. "I promised we would clean it up and get rid of the pear out of the yard. It will be hard work."

Quite amazingly, the ramshackle old house suddenly appeared like the Marriott Hotel – luxury beyond their wildest imaginations. Jo eagerly picked up a stray picket and used it to prise off the boards that barred the door. She wanted to see what it was like inside.

* * *

5

They walked carefully down the dim hallway. It seemed that whoever had lived here had left with very little. There were just two bedrooms at the front of the house. The beds were stripped – the mattresses gone from the steel frames. Two or three mattresses were strewn in disarray. The small sitting room was crowded with a worn grubby lounge heaped with rags that were probably once clothes and other leftover bits and pieces.

Out the back was a semi-detached kitchen. There was not much there – a couple of saucepans, a broken meat safe and old metal box with a few shredded hessian strips hung around the sides. A few plates still sat on the open shelf that had served as a kind of kitchen hutch. In the main house curtains hung in limp, spidery sheets at the windows. Bits of paper and rubbish and dust lay in piles along the hall and in the doorways. Jo bent over and picked up an old celluloid doll. It was bald and missing an arm and a leg. She sat it on a table. Somehow it seemed disrespectful to leave it in the pile of rubbish. It had been someone's much loved companion and spoke of friendlier, more affluent days.

Suddenly Andi stopped. She froze and grabbed Jo's arm. "Rats!" She hissed. "They're everywhere!"

They had been looking at what was left in this little cottage, but now they saw movement… swift and fleeting. A grey fury body buzzed behind the door. Another miraculously ran up the wall and through a hole above the picture rail. Everywhere they looked: a row of tails dangled from the top of a shelf, little eyes cheekily stared them down and ran boldly passed them. Andi felt her knees go wobbly and struggled towards a chair. Rodents. Gross. Not only that - there were millions of them! Their free resort accommodation was a rat's nest! Huhh! She felt her stomach heave and she ran for the front door.

They could never stay here. It was impossible! They would have to go back to the Hotel, until they could get the place exterminated. Jo came out a little while later. "Daisy's taken the bedroom on the left – with the double bed. We have the other one," she said calmly as she handed Andi a handkerchief.

"We can't *stay* here. No way! The place is crawling! They're enormous!"

"Daisy's settled the rooms at the Hotel. This is it."

"We won't be able to sleep or eat or do anything! Oh Jo – I am *not* going back in there! I can't!"

"We'll stay awake then. There's nowhere else to go. Daisy's making a list of things we need. We'll have kero for the lamp, and we'll just sit it out. It won't seem so bad in the light."

"Jo – it *is* light now," said Andi pointing to the high afternoon sun, "and it's not even close to being okay! Nothing could possibly be worse. How could we conceivably survive a whole night here?" She shivered in revulsion.

"We have a few hours to do what we can to get ready. Are you going to help?" asked Jo, now totally unsympathetic to her friend's paranoia.

Andi looked up at her. "I don't think I can Jo. Honestly – I'm totally freaked out. They gnaw off toes and eat your eyes out when you sleep. Surely you know that?"

Jo looked at her seriously terrified face and burst out laughing. "No. Can't say I've *ever* heard that! Andi – they're rats. Not planet-invading human-eating aliens! In case you haven't noticed, we are a million times bigger than they are… and smarter. We'll get rid of them – somehow."

"Go ahead. I'm not going in there."

Jo grunted and went back inside. She was annoyed that Andi would leave her to do their part of the work. Daisy went about her own affairs like a solo pilot. She made no attempt to help or work together – even at Jo's suggestion. She had let them inside the house. Bonus, but they were strangers. The only time Daisy made any effort to communicate was to clearly define boundaries in remote, ice-cold terms. If they went into her room – they were dead. If they touched such and such… they were dead. Jo thought it was all a bit much.

Jo found an old broom with barely any bristles and started sweeping out their bedroom. She poked at a pile of debris and disturbed some rats. Jo squealed in surprise as they scattered in a multi-directional scuffle under the bed, behind the door and through holes in the floor. Huh! Andi was right. They were revolting. But they had to start to do something to make the place habitable.

* * *

Andi sat on the step with her head on her knees. She tried not to think, but every time she closed her eyes images of man-eating rats the size of cows went marauding through the house to attack her! In the end, even sitting on the step was too close to their beady eyes, hairless tails, and malicious buckteeth. She stood up and went for a walk. At the gate, Andi turned away from the main town. She had no desire to be confronted again by unexplainably antagonistic residents.

She walked quickly along the road, passing the constant monotonous conglomerate of prickly pear. Even the trees that perhaps once stood gracefully along the side of the road, were hidden in the giant green masses. Dull birds picked at the red fruit and flew away as she hurried passed. Tears stung her eyes. This was so unbelievably awful. Was there no one who would help them? She was trying to out walk all the feelings that were crowding her in. *Oh God, this is so mean. I don't get it! I just want someone to be nice to me!* Andi threw the accusation at God. Wasn't He in control? Didn't He have all the answers? Wasn't He her special friend? *Great way to show it!* She thought bitterly. Just one pleasant word and then even the rats would not seem so desperate. *'Why can't someone just be kind?'* she asked again – just in case He didn't hear.

Jo is.

'Yeah – but she doesn't count... not really. Everyone else is so horrible to us.'

You have one friend. Some people have no one.

For some reason Andi thought of Daisy. It certainly didn't seem like she had any friends. *'But'*, thought Andi defensively, *'that is all her own doing. She's rude and aloof. Who in their right mind would want to be her friend?'*

I didn't come to gather friends for myself – but to **be** a friend. You could do the same.

Andi stopped walking. It was a rebuke, but not a rebuke. It was like Jesus understood her friendless state and empathised; but not a syllable contained any pity. It was a statement of fact, expectation, directive and coaxing – all thrown in together, and it blew her mind. Andi stood there stunned as she tried to grapple with the truth of what had been spoken. New understanding dawned on her about the well-worn command, "Do for others as you would have them do for you."

Jesus had never been on a friend-finding mission – that was not to say he didn't want companionship or desire care… but *that* need was never the focus. Jesus was always a faithful friend to those few around him, even though he knew one would end up selling his friendship for thirty pieces of silver. Even John – his best, best friend in the whole world, deserted him when he needed his support most of all. And Peter… he couldn't even admit to knowing him. But Jesus didn't just stop there. He was kind to the destitute. He even touched untouchable outcasts and beggars – really touched them, probably even hugged them. Jesus was their friend. He may not have spent hours and years with them – yet he was their friend in the moment, as he passed by.

The words burnt into her heart: *'Go and do the same…"* Her? That was the single most difficult thing God had ever asked of her. Be a friend… to obnoxious loud travellers with nasty little sons? Or Daisy – cold, distant Daisy? Or the man at the shop: who unexplainably had an aversion to loiterers? Or the lady who yelled at them, when she didn't even know them? How do you be a friend to people like that?

'Well', thought Andi. 'I can start with Jo, I guess. If I can't be a good friend to my best friend, there is no hope of doing it to all the other hard cases around here.' Andi knew that meant helping her clean up and confronting the rats. Honestly that terrified her. They may be only little – no, let's be honest: they were really huge… and there were so many! How could Kenny Watts, the class computer-nerd at her school, ever have one as a pet. He brought it to class one day, and it sat on his shoulder as he worked at the computer station. The idea was incredibly nauseating, but it gave her insight that the species may not be as malevolent or ferocious as she had thought.

She turned around, and determinedly walked back towards the cottage, praying as she went. Jesus – please help me. I want to be a good friend… I want to… but I don't think I can if you don't help me. Show us how to get rid of the rats. I have no experience with a pest problem like this."

Andi had no idea she had walked so far. Suddenly she looked around and tried to remember coming this way. The prickly-pear made everything look the same, and a glow of alarm started to grow in her belly. Was she headed further into the back blocks of no-where? She kept walking, thinking for sure that soon something would seem familiar. Nothing did. As she turned the next corner, she saw a man with a hoe, shovel and string line working on the side of the road. He waved congenially as she went passed.

Perhaps it was because he was the first person to seem relatively pleasant in Gum Ridge, or maybe just because the panic of being lost was about to set in, but Andi stopped when he tipped his beat up old felt hat cordially and said, "Good afternoon, ma'am."

"Hi," said Andi. "I don't remember coming past here. Is this the way back to town?"

"Sure – next bend. Nearly there."

"Oh." Andi felt she wanted to say something else, but he didn't seem the chatty type. "Well, thank you. I appreciate it. I was starting to get a bit panicky that I had made a wrong turn."

"You seemed pretty preoccupied when you went by before."

"Oh, I'm sorry – I didn't even see you."

"New here… heh?"

"Yeah… came on the train the day before yesterday. Never even knew Gum Ridge existed before we arrived. Why do they call it Gum Ridge anyway? I haven't even seen a gumtree. Should be called Prickly Hollow!" Andi smiled at her own little joke. The residents were true to that name anyway.

The man smiled a quiet sort of grin. "There's ridge

out on Murray's place. There's a gum or two over that way. Pretty sure."

Andi laughed. The understated observation was so refreshing! "Well if I am as close as you say, that tumble-down house around the corner is our new home. We've just moved in. It's a total dump and overrun with rats. I'm not good with vermin. I'm gathering courage to go back and face the pestilence."

He paused for a long time. Andi wasn't sure if he was surprised or just not sure what to say. He took off his hat and wiped the sweat from his brow. He replaced his hat carefully, as if it took a great deal of thought. "Oh," he said noncommittally.

"The house is the pits and totally falling to pieces," continued Andi as if his mono-syllable reply was a green light to continue... "but it's free rent... which helps."

Harry raised his eyebrows thoughtfully. He said nothing and Andi continued. Three days of not talking to anyone besides Jo had made her quite chatty. "Daisy said she was able to make an agreement with the landlord so we can stay there if we clean it up. We can have it as long as we need on those terms while she's out of work. But it beats me how we are ever going to get rid of the rats." In saying that, Andi suddenly realised that someone, somewhere had been kind to them already. She felt sorry for her unfair accusations.

"Daisy? You're with Daisy Brown?"

"Yeah – you know her?"

"A long time ago," he said quietly.

"It seems that everyone knows her – but no one wants to *know* her – if you get what I mean. It's like we've been hit with the scarlet fever and everyone is so totally…"

He smiled calmly; his brown eyes creased kindly at the corners. "Bush telegraph – very efficient, but not always accurate."

Andi paused and looked at the man. "Sorry – I was not being real fair. But I just don't get it. Daisy's not the easiest person to get along with, I know that, but …. Anyway, it's all a bit strange really – how we got to be here, but well, here we are… rats and all."

He grinned. "Welcome to Gum Ridge."

"Huh – some welcome. We hardly hit town, and people everywhere seemed to know Daisy's back… but it's like she's blacklisted. When we went asking for work today – so we could pay our way… no one wanted anything to do with us."

"Times are hard…"

With a flash of insight Andi said, "People are hard! Just because we are with Daisy no one wants to give us a chance. What could she have possibly done that was so horrendous?"

Harry took his hat off again and carefully wiped his brow. "I'm looking to build a mechanical shop," he said as if it was completely related to the current flow of conversation. He waved to the patch he had cleared behind him.

"Out here?" said Andi with surprise.

"It's near the road…"

"Yeah – but wouldn't it be better to have it near the town as well?"

"It is… just around the corner."

"Well, you know that, and I know that… *now*. But no one just driving through is going to know that. You need to be seen!" Andi suddenly laughed. "Sorry. I've just given advice to a man I don't know, about a business I don't know, in a place I don't know. Hope it was extremely helpful!"

He seemed unperturbed. He just smiled. "Well, I can correct one of those. My name is Harry Dunn." He stuck out his hand.

Andi grabbed it enthusiastically… "Pleased to meet you Harry. My name is Andrea… Andi." She paused. "Well, I best be getting back. Jo will be trying to work out how to rid that horrendous little hovel of all those rats. I feel much braver now. Thanks for talking."

"No problem. You should get some proper boots for walking though, – not those little shoes. Snakes are thick 'round here… especially death adders. They lie in the dirt and ya can step on them without knowin'."

Andi stared at him, trying to tell if he was spinning her a yarn as some perverted bush joke, but his brown eyes were quiet and sincere. She turned on her heel and ran back to the house as fast as she could.

Andi bowled through the door. "There is nowhere in this place that is safe. There are rats inside, and snakes outside! Jo! I'll do anything – just tell me what needs to be done. I'm not going to look at them – I'm just going to try and help you… so quick – give me something to do before I lose my nerve!" The rats were now definitely the lesser of two evils.

Jo was relieved. "This is the most disgusting place I've ever seen. We need a place to sleep tonight. I've emptied the room and swept the floor. Daisy's busy using bits of rag to clog up holes so I've started doing that as well."

She presented Andi with a long wick of thick rag to ram down the holes in the floor… and skirting board… and walls… and windowsills. Every knothole in the timber was potentially a doorway for a rat… or God forbid – a snake! Even the little holes, too small for a cockroach, got plugged

– just in case.

Then they moved the iron bed frames back into the room. They looked at the mattresses that were left. One had a kind of hard straw filling that was held together by striped fabric ticking. Leather buttons punched dints all the way down the mattress. The only other mattress that seemed half decent had kapok stuffing - an off-white cotton-type of wadding that disintegrated in powdery puffs and made Andi sneeze. Both of them had large holes in their fabric covers and looked very much like they had been the dual-residence of the 'rat-family of prickly-hollow' for a very long time.

They banged and thumped on the stuffing and were debating how to be sure there were still no rats in the mattresses when there was a knock at the door. Jo looked at Andi, Andi looked at the door. When she opened it, Harry stood there with some enamel plates in one hand, and a couple of broom handles with twisted wire attached to the end, in the other hand. "Brought you a couple of snake-sticks... and some poison... for the rats.

"Snake sticks?" said Andi dubiously, looking at the rather unusual contraption in his hand.

"Yeah – it pays to have a couple around handy... you just never know when you'll need it. Wire don't snap when you thump them... sticks'll break – every time." He leant the sticks up against the front door and held up the plates. "Baits'll take a while to work… but should do the trick."

"You can bait rats?" asked Andi.

Harry looked at her curiously. They obviously were fish out of water; walking along the dirt road in court shoes told him that. He nodded. "Got a trap as well…"

"Baits? We have no money to pay you…." Andi informed him dubiously. Harry shrugged unconcerned. "Traps?" she said, "Like a snap, break your neck – we have to empty it and set it again, sort of trap?"

Jo elbowed her way to the door to check out who would be talking so agreeably with Andi. It had her intrigued there were no raised voices, no icy glares.

"I'll put out the baits and then set the trap. Can come by and empty it in the morning. That'll spare you the need."

"Hate to be disagreeable when you're being so thoughtful," said Jo, "but aren't you just being a tad optimistic to think that one trap will cure the problem here? There are millions of them! Oh – by the way, I'm Jo."

"Your name is Joe?" He was obviously surprised.

"Yeah – short for Josephine. Jo. No 'e'."

"Pleased to meet you Jo: Harry Dunn," said Harry with a twist of humour on his mouth. *Green to the core*, he confirmed to himself.

Daisy emerged from her room then, her blonde hair

mussed, and her face smeared with grime. The front of her dress was wet and dirty from scrubbing the floor. She had a bucket in her arms and was on her way out the back to get a fresh lot of water from the tank. She caught the sight of them standing in the doorway from the corner of her eye. She stopped abruptly. Water sloshed from her bucket and drenched the front of her dress. She muttered something under her breath, as she put down the bucket and looked at the intruder.

"Welcome home Daisy," said Harry quietly.

Daisy cheeks were already flushed, but the sight of someone catching her so unrehearsed was something she was not prepared for. Always the actress, suddenly Daisy was caught without a costume. It didn't sit well with her.

"Harry?"

"Nice to have you back," he said sincerely.

Daisy certainly didn't feel at home. "Humph!" she grunted. She grabbed her bucket and fled out the back. Harry looked after her thoughtfully.

Jo smiled sarcastically. "Don't mind Daisy. Her warm heart is hidden under deep layers of swish clothes, polished good manners and cool social graces."

"I'll set the baits," said Harry as he removed his hat. "It'll stink some when they start to die," he said matter-of-factly.

"Oh great," groaned Andi. But if she had to choose between live rats and dead ones, dead ones were certainly preferable. Harry went up into the ceiling and poked around under the house. He went outside to where his horse and farm cart stood by the fence and put away the lantern, he had used to find his way around the ceiling. Harry thought he would not bother mentioning they had three very long, sleek carpet snakes residing in the ceiling rafters. The news of more wildlife would not be thrilling news to these girls, he suspected. Nor would he tell them he had decided against putting any baits out. Those pythons were better pest-control than most. He'd hate to see them suffer because their food was poisoned.

"Where do you want the trap?" he asked when he came back in.

"I don't know – kitchen maybe… don't want rats in the kitchen."

"What about…" he paused. "Maybe the main part of the house to start with? Can move it tomorrow if you want." Jo and Andi shrugged. One rat in the lounge or the kitchen was not going to make that much difference. They wouldn't be resetting it during the night… that was for sure.

Harry had brought in a large wooden barrel from the cart – the kind Andi had seen in movies to store wine in cellars. The top had been removed. He had a coil of rope over his shoulder, and a loaf of stale bread in a bag.

Andi looked perplexed. "Haven't you got one of those little mouse trap things, with a spring – only bigger… like rat-size?"

"Nope."

"How is this going to trap rats?" asked Jo, always the humourist. "Feed them to death?"

"You'll see," said Harry noncommittally. He went to work. He placed the barrel in the middle of the room. He strung the rope from the top of one wooden chair to another, over the top of the barrel. He asked Andi to fill the bottom of the barrel with water. Then he took some finer rope and slashed it around the half loaf of bread like a fish net and hung it over the middle of the barrel, so it dangled above the water. "There," said Harry when he had finished. "This works well for mice. Never done it for rats – but it should work much the same, I should think."

"That's it?" said Andi sceptically. "How's *that* going to work?"

When Harry was explaining what he was familiar with, he suddenly became quite verbose. "A rat will climb anything for food. The bread attracts them. They'll smell it a mile away. They run out along the rope to get to the bread. And then they'll run down this rope to the bread, some of them will lose their balance and drop into the barrel. The barrel has curved sides so they shouldn't be able to climb out of it... before they drown, anyway. That's the theory.

"Errhhh! That's barbaric!"

"The brutality of being over-run. You could always try and co-exist."

"Oh no! The barrel is fine," said Andi quickly.

"Like I said... haven't actually set this for rats. There's a mouse version that everyone knows – with a bottle and cheese and a bucket. By morning we'll know if it works or needs a few adjustments."

Jo was looking at it quite amazed. "In the light of that, it's quite ingenious," she conceded. "Harry, just one thing though... what if it works?"

"Less rats. That's the plan."

"But..."

He looked at her and waited... "But what?" he eventually prompted.

"Well – if it works, we are going to have a barrel full of rats! What are we going to do with that?"

* * *

6

Amazingly – they survived the first night, and the second. True to his word Harry came and reset the rat-barrel and disposed of the seething mass of fur and teeth at the bottom. Tallying their haul became a game. Any sympathy the girls might have had for the rodents was amazingly short lived. At night they would hear a rustle and a splosh as another hit the bottom of the barrel, and they would roll over and say "Bingo!" In just over one week their nightly tally was regularly reducing and they were winning the battle.

The girls found some old boots in a cupboard and cleaned and oiled them so they could go walking along the road, just to get out of the house. Andi showed Jo where Harry planned to build his Mechanical work-shed, but she noticed that no further progress on the block had been made. Prickly-pear was already growing back on the small area he had cleared.

"Hope what I said didn't put you off," said Andi when she realised, he seemed to have abandoned the project altogether.

He simply said, "Thought about what you said. Asked the boss… just waiting for a reply." Well, they couldn't argue with that.

One afternoon, Andi dragged Jo into the lounge room and they accosted Daisy together. She was lying listlessly on the lounge reading a magazine. It was a new publication for women, and Daisy had read it numerous times already. "We'd like to make a list of things that we need to do so that all the stuff for the house gets done."

She barely looked at them. "You're just kids. What do you care if the work gets done?" she said through the pages of her mag'. "If you're bored, take up dancing or something…"

Andi's glare burnt holes through the pages that covered Daisy's face. "I'm not bored," she said defensively. "I care because that was the agreement. You said we had the house rent-free as long as we tidied up. The house isn't much, but it's better than being without a house at all."

Daisy ignored them and went on reading, mechanically fiddling with the ring on her hand.

Andi took a breath and continued her speech. "We haven't even started on the yard and there is still a heap we could do inside. That was the deal. It was pretty generous and we should keep our end of the bargain."

Daisy turned another page.

"Daisy!"

"What?" she said impatiently.

"We have a contract to fulfil... we need to all chip in."

"There was no deal," Daisy said irritably.

"Just because it wasn't written down, doesn't make it any less valid. We have to keep our word."

Daisy looked as if she was going to say something, but then sighed and closed her magazine and sat up. "Unbelievable," she muttered. "I got stuck with the only two teenagers in the world with a conscience."

Now that they had Daisy's attention, Jo was keen to add her piece. "I reckon we should just do house-stuff in the morning, and then we can have the afternoons to ourselves."

Daisy nodded. "Sounds good to me."

"But," Andi objected, "If there are things that need to be done..."

"Vote," said Daisy quickly. Jo and Daisy put up their hands. "Carried," said Daisy with finality. "Now you wanted a list? Write down every room in the house and the outside yard. Okay. Done. Meeting closed." She lay back down and opened her magazine again. Andi glared at her. Daisy glanced over the top of the pages. "We'll start tomorrow. It's already afternoon."

* * *

Harry sat with his father at the table as his mother

dished up the evening meal. Harry never lost the habit ground into him from his childhood, of sitting quietly until dinner was served. An onlooker could have possibly thought it chauvinistic – that the men would sit and expect to be waited on, but it would have been an affront to Mrs Dunn's abilities as a wife and mother if one offered help in the kitchen. This was her domain, and she was intensely territorial when it came to household matters. It was her personal unchallenged conviction that men did the outside work; her business pertained to the house, and 'never the twain should meet'.

Finally, Mrs Dunn settled wordlessly into the chair beside her husband, and bowed her head. They all clasped hands in a uniform gesture. Mr Dunn quietly gave thanks to God for the provision of their meal. It was short and to the point. They murmured 'Amen'. Wordlessly, Mrs Dunn passed the gravy boat. The sauce was thin and watery, but they lavished it on their potatoes as if it was the way it used to be when times were more prosperous.

"They've called a meeting at the hall next Tuesday. Some fellows have come up with another solution for the pear," said Mr Dunn.

The news was acknowledged with a nod. Another plan… but no offer of hope. Mrs Dunn cleared her throat. It was a tradition to use meal-times as a forum for discussion – in a monosyllabic Dunn-kind-of-way. "How are the new tenants going?" She was addressing Harry, but he didn't seem to register. "Harry… the Muldoon cottage," she said more directly. The old house was still known as *The Muldoon Cottage*. That was a more accurate address than saying it was on South Street.

Harry looked up. "Oh. Well enough."

"Son, the place isn't decent. It's been vacant for years."

"Uhuh," he affirmed. "Had a problem with rats." He continued to chew on a tough over-stewed piece of meat. All its flavour had long been boiled away.

"I just don't know why you didn't tell us," his mother said. "It could have been quite embarrassing – if we had gone up there not knowing you had arranged the whole thing."

Harry said nothing, but carefully pushed his meat into the gravy. It dawned on him that his parents knew no more about Daisy moving in than he did. He murmured an apology. His father wordlessly sawed off a slice of bread as if he was hacking into a fallen tree for firewood.

Mrs Dunn was not finished. "Now I don't abide gossip, but that girl has a bad reputation."

Harry pursed his lips and said nothing.

"And her hangers on… they can't be up to any good

– living like that. They should have waited until it was cleaned up some," she said grimly.

"Had nowhere else to go… guess that's why they didn't wait."

She grunted quietly and said, "I'm not at all surprised. What terms did you agree on?"

Harry slowly chewed his mouthful. He wanted to measure his words. He wasn't about to lie, but he figured his parents had enough to worry about without adding to it the knowledge that Daisy had moved in on her own volition. "The place is a dump," said Harry quoting Andi. He smiled to himself over her innocent declaration. He'd only met them a few days ago, but he figured she would have chosen her words more carefully, had she known she was talking to her landlord. "They'll clean it up some... and that can be the rent for now. That'll save me. Otherwise, it'll just finish fallin' down."

Mrs Dunn bristled. "The Muldoon's were a respected family in this town. I'll not tolerate their home being used in the Devil's work."

Harry continued eating. His father quietly spread dripping on his bread. "Now Margaret, you know the deed is in Harry's name. He can rent it to whomever he wishes."

"Yes, but everyone knows…"

"I'll keep an eye on them Ma. I'm changing the site

of the workshop to Muldoon's horse paddock next to the cottage. Closer to town seems a better idea. I've seen the councillors. They're okay with it."

Mr Dunn studied his bread as he cut it into squares and systematically sopped up his gravy with his knife and fork. He didn't pause or look up when he spoke. "Penfield thinks you've lost your marbles in the Big Smoke, Son. He came to see me about your application. Gum Ridge will never support a workshop like that."

"Councillor Penfield thinks putting grease on his axle and feeding his horse is progress... but Pa, that's just maintenance. We need progress. It'll come... and when it does – I'll be ready."

"Now Harry, common sense tells me-and-you-both, that those motorised carriages will never come to the country... not in a big way. They're a city fad Son, that's all," his father concluded.

"Doctor Larsen has one. Telford's are getting one too, coming next month. I'll do blacksmithing jobs until work comes regular."

"Big smoke Wannabe's... that's all they are. You know I reckon this workshop is a scare-brain crazy idea. Still - you're not out robbing banks, so I reckon ya could do worse."

"I appreciate your concern Pa. It'll be okay." Mr

Dunn looked at his son with a mixture of pride and confusion. His calm unrelenting confidence that "it'll be okay" was beyond his comprehension. Like he said – at least Harry wasn't in trouble with the Law. Plenty of the town's young'ns – those few who came back from the war, had selected their farms in the Government's war-veterans scheme. It was to be their lifeline – a reward for their war effort. But they'd lost the plot when it became evident their farms were too small to support them and then they were over-run with the Prickly Pear Curse. It was too much trauma on top of trauma. Harry hadn't lost it though. His faith was a stabilising bar. He just didn't waiver much. Mr Dunn thanked God daily that his Harry had been young enough to be drafted late and never saw active duty.

* * *

Andi stood with a bucket in her hand. It had rust holes in the side, so it leaked if she filled it more than halfway. Jo threw her a rag. "There's a hole in your bucket, Dear Liza, Dear Liza…" she chanted in a sing-song voice.

Andi was not impressed. She wondered how she could ever fix up a house without the proper stuff. A mop would help. "I think we should start at the front of the house and work back and then do the yard last of all."

Jo shrugged, "So that means we start on the verandah today… it will take more than one day to do this you know."

"Okay – let's work out what we need to do." Andi looked at the lattice falling off in bits.

"We can't salvage that... look – it's rotted through! What are we going to do with it?" Jo directed her question to Daisy who stood back with a very tired and bored expression.

Daisy shrugged. She felt numb. Gum Ridge was sucking the life out of her. She missed singing; she missed the stage; she missed acting; she missed being important. She even missed her city-friends... even though she knew most of them were honestly more interested in the popular publicity she generated than what she felt or thought. But still, even superficial acquaintances who think you're useful in a career move, are preferable to an aggressive populace who hate the ground you stand on. It seemed hard to remember why she ever came back to Gum Ridge. The dilapidated lattice and rotting boards on the verandah represented exactly how she felt. She wanted to be left alone to rot away in peace. But peace was not what she had. Anything but. She shrugged again. "Dunno – burn it for all I care."

"Hey! We could take all the junk and pile it in one spot – then we could do just that! We'll have a huge bon-fire as a grand finalé when we're finished. There'll be heaps more junk that needs to be burnt."

Daisy's gaze took a cynical sweep over the pile of debris in the corner. "We should just torch the whole place and be done with it."

Andi was getting jack of her listless, sarcastic comments. She made everything so much harder than it had to be. Sure, it wasn't great… but it was what they had to work with. Daisy was supposed to be the grown-up here… but she wasn't acting like it. Andi felt she was being pushed into taking responsibility because no one else would. She hated it! She wanted her mother to come and tell her what to do; to give her a job and make sure she did it. She wanted her Mum to cook her favourite chicken dinner and then pile her bowl with ice-cream and waffles for dessert, and then let her off the washing up because she had an assignment due. This grown-up thing was not all it was cracked up to be. Did it have any pay-offs at all? Was it as inevitable as your next birthday and as miserable as Daisy's attitude? Well – who'd want it?

Andi looked at Daisy standing slouched and bored and cynical by the verandah post in a crushed, grubby dress. Jo was staring vacantly at a red-back spider playing with a white ball of web in the recesses of the cracks between the weather-boards. Andi figured she had no choice. Well, that is not exactly true. She could choose to join their pointless apathy... or she could choose to make a start. If nothing else, doing *something* would be better than spending her time doing nothing and have everything stay the same. She had no idea who the landlord was, but Daisy had made a tenancy agreement, and one day he would come and inspect the house. If he saw they had not made any attempt to tidy up as they had agreed, they could be evicted and have literally nowhere to live.

Andi decided then, that even if Jo and Daisy were going to waste away, she would make this work. "God – this is so unfair... we should do this together. But even if they're not going to help, I will start. But I'm just saying up front I'm not sure how I'll be able to keep going."

She wordlessly pulled down the lattice and piled it in a heap on the verandah. She picked up the boards and wove her way through the prickly pear in the front yard and dumped her load over the fence. She went back and piled splinters and rubbish into her bucket and dumped that too. She went inside and found the broom and swept up blown leaves and rubbish that accumulated in the corner.

Suddenly Daisy lunged forward and pulled her back. "Stop it!" said Andi impatiently swinging around at her. "Look, I know you don't care. I also know you don't want to do anything to help fix this place up... but you have no right to stop me from trying to do the right thing."

Jo quietly turned Andi's shoulder and pointed a shaky finger at the corner of the verandah. The smooth sleek tail of a brown coloured snake was disappearing through a crack in the floorboards. It had been in the pile of stuff that Andi was about to pick up. Andi let out a terrified scream and ran inside slamming her bedroom door, bolting it shut. She stood there, hysterically screaming and screaming and screaming. Panic squeezing her senses. She lost track of everything except the terror of being so close to death.

Jo came in and banged on the bedroom door. "Andi! It's me. Will you open the door? You're okay. You're okay!" she said, trying to get Andi to calm down and listen. But it is doubtful Andi heard anything above her hysteria.

Daisy carefully shut the front door, and wadded rolls of rags against the crack underneath the door. She shrugged. "Heard they flatten out… and can get in under small spaces," she said looking at the snake-sticks Harry had left.

Jo had no idea how to kill a snake, and she trembled a little. It felt like they were being made hostage in their own house by all sorts of threats. It wasn't just people who were out to make life a prison. Anger started to rise inside her that was stronger than the numbing daze that was paralysing her like a death adder's venom. No living thing had the right to do that to her! No longer was she going to

lie down and let it happen. Her fighting spirit reared up.
She would show them! They would clean this place up and
they would win.

* * *

7

Harry paused to offer his Mother an elbow to lean on as she walked up the stairs of the community hall. His father followed with a small basket of morning tea. Their offering seemed so meagre compared to the days when they would come laden with more stuff than an army could eat. She hustled out to the side room of the hall to help some ladies ready the morning tea. Normally their preparations would be filled with chatter and socialising. Today the ladies wordlessly went about arranging cups and plates, mumbling the odd apology when they bumped into each other. Mavis Larsen, the doctor's wife, came in from outside where she had been filling the billies ready to put on the fire once the meeting was over.

Margaret Dunn looked wordlessly at her friends. She felt for them. She quietly went over to Mrs Larsen. "Mavis – it was good of you to come by to help. I know these meetings... well, they're not directly affecting you."

"Oh Margaret – how can you say that? This impacts all of us. The district means everything to Arthur and me. He was hoping to get here, but old Mrs Grayson needed a house-call. He might come later... although he said he would drop into the Bennett's on his way home."

"I didn't mean to imply…." She sighed. "It's just farming business that's all. Your support means a lot. It seems so pointless really." Margaret Dunn very rarely got so down but as she looked at the dwindling numbers of fighters, she found it harder and harder to stir herself. How many more meetings? How many times could the promises cause hope to be punched out of her friends? How many more tears needed to be cried in the face of unrelenting tragedy?

Two young men in suits sat at the front of the hall. There was an easel with a diagram of the cactus clipped to it and the contents of a couple of suitcases were lined up on the table. Margaret pursed her lips. *The average farmer actually knows what a cactus looks like,* she thought cynically. *Do they think we are simpletons?*

She shuffled down beside her husband and son, as Councillor Penfield got up and cleared his throat. "We'll get started friends. Would like to thank you for coming. These two are from the Prickly Pear Board and they want a few words." Gone were the days when he would try and give an upbeat introduction. He wanted facts, just like his neighbours. He nodded and sat down. A few murmured that they hoped it would not take too long. A wagonload of work always awaited them.

Mr Wallis stood and adjusted his collar. He wished

they had not been expected to wear a suit by the department. Even though all the locals had come to the meeting in their town clothes, his coat and tie automatically hung a placard that labelled them townies, academics, failures… those who could not make it in the real world of farming, and so resorted to books. Mr Wallis's loved the land and these people had no idea about his own family's rural tragedy. He understood what pear was doing and his experience motivated him to help bring this invasion under control. No one ever asked him and he was not pushy enough to volunteer the information.

It seemed impossible that some lovingly tended potted ornamental from the 1830's could become the undoing of a nation. Yet the cactus was doing just that – choking out productivity by the throat. They needed solutions: economical, safe measures - a natural predator that would eat this invincible weed from the inside out. Now they had it. The years of research and travel to the Americas investigating options had eventually paid off. They were finally able to release the moth – the cactoblastis moth. At last, they had something that was a tangible hope. Mr Wallis looked over at his colleague, who sat flicking his pencil. He was anxious to start. He thought they were playing the part of heroes coming to save these people from destruction.   It   was   beyond   his   companion's comprehension that they would not be welcomed with open arms.

Mr Wallis cleared his throat. The murmurings persisted. The sombre atmosphere was subtly changing to a disgruntled anger. Mr Wallis was aware he represented someone they could blame for their problems. "Ladies and Gentlemen, the Prickly Pear Board has sent us to explain the next phase in their strategy for controlling prickly pear." Some derisive grunts filtered around the fringes. He took a deep breath and continued. "As you know, we have been researching for the best way to bring it under control. Chemicals have proven too expensive and too ineffective... not to mention the health issues that seem to be constantly under debate in connection with them. The Commission has believed now for a number of years that a natural means of containment would be most beneficial. I can inform you today that we have found a natural control. Our studies confirm that it is safe. It will only attack pest-pear. We are ready to release it." He was becoming excited. He knew what this meant – it meant relief, and he paused dramatically.

Councillor Penfield offered a few half-hearted claps and a couple of others joined in. Most were past being polite. A voice from the back spoke up. "So, what is it? A chant and a wand... read it, wave it and poof!!!" He guffawed loudly at his own joke. A few of his neighbours did too. There was precious little to laugh about now-a-days. Mr Wallis's ears tinged red. They enjoyed his discomfort for a while before settling down. Councillor Penfield smiled and then quickly ducked his head to hide his impropriety.

Mr Wallis didn't blame them for their scepticism. The track record of the 'Prickly Pear Destruction Commission' was poor as far as the locals could see. How do you measure the significance of long days of tedious laboratory work? It seemed they had done nothing to destroy pear, and quite a bit to annihilate good will and faith. But now they had something that was real: today they would get something they could see and hold and do. Mr Wallis felt a touch of pride that today was a direct result of the persistent hard work of his colleagues and himself.

"Actually – it is almost as simple. A moth: Cactoblastis cactorum." He stepped over to the easel and flipped over the page. The life cycle of a non-descript insect, with an orange, black spotted grub, was featured on the next sheet. He continued quickly. "This moth is an Argentinean species. Its larvae feed exclusively on pest-pear. This diagram is what happens to the spongy pear stems when the larvae eat it out. They become hollow and disintegrate." He quickly flipped to the next page. A rather poor drawing showed a prickly pear picture with unconvincing black splodges over it. A restless scraping of chairs made Mr Wallis realise he was losing their attention. He cut to the chase. "The Commission will supply quills containing the Cactoblastis eggs to property owners. We have the quills with us. The procedure is simple and quick. All you need to do is to stab the straws into the flesh of the Prickly pear. Choose areas where the pear is thick and virulent…"

Someone muttered under his breath, "You ain't got *that* many quills…."

Mr Wallis pulled out his handkerchief and wiped his brow. He had not anticipated that the results of the last four years of his life would be greeted with such scorn, not to mention the countless years in man-hours accumulated by those who worked on the project with him. It was very hard not to take it personally. "It can take up to a month for the eggs to hatch. I assure you gentlemen, after that there will be visible results very soon. We'll have a question time now. Then you can come and give us your details as you collect the quills.

There were very few questions. More interest was generated by the knowledge that the billy had been put on to boil out the back of the hall, than this newest scientific solution. Some of the young ones finally escaped and ran down to the water-hole behind the hall. You could hear the whoops of released pent-up energy as they swung wildly out over the water on a knotted rope, jumping and splashing in the creek. Their exuberant fun made a peculiar contrast to the atmosphere in the hall. The ladies quietly congratulated each other's scones. They piled on prickly pear jam and passed them around. The men stood about in clusters bemoaning the fate that had been dealt them. Very soon the morning tea was over. Everyone went their own way, a few quills poking carelessly from their pockets. That was over, and they went back to the monotony of their hard lives.

Harry stayed to help shut the windows in the hall. He paused as the suit-men were packing their things. "Appreciate your efforts," he said with a nod.

Mr Wallis looked as if he hadn't heard correctly. No accusations or sarcastic asides? He responded warmly. "This is going to work you know."

Harry was no more convinced of the virtues of this new strategy than anyone else. He just was more polite perhaps. "Sure. Here let me help you with your stuff." He grabbed a bag and went with them to the door.

"Listen – not as many turned up as we expected… here – have some extra quills… it'll give you a chance to get different areas of your place covered more quickly." Mr

Wallis reached out and shook his hand. "Good luck mate."

Harry went out to where his parents were waiting in the sulky. One quill was sticking conspicuously out of a prickly pear by the fence. A few more quills lay scattered on the ground. He quickly picked them up out of embarrassment. He could easily dispose of them at home. It would be shameful for the men to see them lying there. Harry believed that good manners were an investment in respect... and *that* was an investment in people. Regardless how tough things were, people should always be treated with respect.

The ride home seemed to take forever. Harry couldn't understand why this community meeting was different from the millions of others that had been conducted at the hall. Yet it was. Perhaps it was just the way Mr Wallis shook his hand as they were leaving and said, 'Good luck'. It seemed genuine, like he really cared about what was happening out here, miles away from his books and laboratory samples. He dismissed it as they drove up the paddock to their house. Common Pear. Pest-Pear. Prickly-Pear. It was more like a jungle than a desert cactus. *God – you said it was going to be okay!* But this time Harry was not reminding himself about what had been promised, it was an accusation hurled into space. God hadn't been faithful after all.

He felt listless and for once instead of tackling the mountains of never-ending tasks, Harry tossed the quills in the bin and went and lay down on his bunk. He picked up his Bible. It was something he did when he felt unsettled. He turned to the Old Testament. He could always find a prayer in The Psalms that was an honest cry to God when things were off centre. He knew he was angry. God was not unfaithful. He was incensed at the unfairness and frustrated at being stuck with no solutions. Harry mumbled an apology as he flicked through the pages, stopping to read a few words now and then. He was doing what he called Scripture grazing… nibbling instead of sitting down to a full three-course Bible-study meal. He found himself reading the story of Naaman[i]… in his mind he translated the stiff formal English, so it sounded as if a friend was telling him a really top story. That's how he liked to think about God: his friend who would tell him a ripping good yarn… and that story always had a point.

Naaman was a commander in the Aramean army: important man, with an important job – rich and famous in Syrian circles – high up the society ladder. But he had one problem: he was sick… in fact: really crook. Terminal… but slow. If this disease went according to the average prognosis, it would not be long before he would lose his job, his home, his family – everything.

Naaman had a slave girl; a wisp of a child who had been included in the spoils of a victorious battle against some Jewish community. It was remarkable that the little kid, bereft of her own family because of this man's command, had whispered to his wife that there was a Hebrew prophet named Elisha who could heal sick people. Naaman's hope began to soar. Perhaps this would be the answer to his no-win situation. He gathered together a diplomatic delegation, and included in his entourage, wagons of treasures to buy this religious man's favour. He was rich – he could pay his way. Then with letters of ambassadorial referral, he went to the King of Israel.

The King was horrified when this Naaman fellow turns up expecting to be healed of his leprosy. The King of Israel was sure the Aramean Army Commander was trying to pick a fight, agitating to start war with his country – again! Didn't he already have captive-slaves from the land of Israel working in his household? But the prophet Elisha heard about the King's panic and sent a message to him and said, "Don't lose the plot – just send the Army bloke on to me…"

So Naaman picked up his contingent and moved over to Elisha's place. Elisha sent out his servant with a message: if he wanted to be healed, all he had to do was go and wash in the Jordan River seven times.

Now fair go... this was a pretty low call. The prophet didn't acknowledge his wagon-load of money, or his many support staff, or his illustrious medals. The very least he should do was to step outside his hut in his prophetic camel hair robes and wave his holy hand over his blotchy leprous skin and chant magic prayers. But he didn't - he just sent a servant with a message. But not only that – what a degrading message! Wash in the run-of-the-mill, weedy, muddy, puny Jordan River... more like a creek really! No way! Naaman went off in a gigantic huff. He was the commander of the world's political super-power... and he was sulking like a girl.

His servants had seen their master in action. No battle was too fierce, no challenge too difficult. They said to him, "Now listen, oh great one... if the guy had asked you to do an impossible feat of daring, skill or bravery – you would have killed yourself trying (and saved us all a lot of trouble)... but because he gave you something uncomplicated and simple, you get ticked off and don't want a bar of it. You'd go to great lengths to do something clever and heroic that might help... why not do something as simple as a wash in a creek?" The satisfying result of this story was that Naaman listened to his staff and washed seven times in the run-of-the-mill, weedy, muddy, puny Jordan River that was more like a creek. God healed

Naaman and he went home healthy.

Harry closed his bible. His paraphrased version amused him, but an expression stuck in his mind: "You'd go to great lengths to do something clever that might help… *why not* do something simple…"

Why not?

Why not?

Parallels began to form in Harry's mind. Parallels like – he was in a desperate fix just like Naaman. If their situation went according to the expected course of events, they would lose everything too. They had done a lot of things – hard, strenuous and difficult things to try and fix their problem. Now a messenger was sent – and the message was simple: stick a quill in a cactus. Was he going to go off in a huff because it wasn't clever or sweaty or impressively painful? Or would he listen to the advice? *Why not…do the simple thing?*

Harry bounded off his bunk and raced out to the kitchen. His Mother was taking the rubbish out. "Wait Ma", he called. He took the bucket and rummaged through the scraps and retrieved all of the quills. In some way he suspected that this time, if he listened to the advice, it was going to make a difference.

* * *

8

Daisy woke up startled. Andi was sitting on her bed stroking her fair hair. Her heart was racing. She felt afraid, and unable to move. She had this nightmare countless of times before, where she had come out of the backstage room, gone onto stage and then realised she had forgotten to dress. She always woke up sweating before she found her clothes. Daisy sat up and pulled herself away from Andi's touch. "I'm all right," she said defensively. "Go back to bed." It seemed to her that Andi had laughed and hooted with the crowded audience in her dream. That was everyone's reaction to seeing someone so exposed and vulnerable.

Andi went back and sat on Jo's bed and drew her knees right to her chin, with her feet curled underneath her. She just wanted to be close to someone. Andi could not actually say she had been woken up by her own nightmare, but she felt hot and sweaty and tired, and she couldn't go back to sleep. She had heard Daisy cry out and gone into her room. As Andi sat on the bed, she couldn't believe she felt so tired. It was like she had just run an official 26.2-mile marathon. Andi hated running so she suspected her tiredness was not related to nocturnal athletic pursuits. Jo reached up and gave Andi a hug. Friends were pretty good. Andi liked the way Jo didn't make her feel stupid for being scared. She wished Daisy could understand that's what friends were like.

Andi had not seen the snake since that day she started to clean up the verandah, but she knew it was still around... somewhere. That thought gave her the creeps. She shuddered. Rats and reptiles: life could not get more hideous than this. The funny thing was, the rats suddenly seemed quite manageable. They still had to lock everything away in metal tins, otherwise they would wake up in the morning to a mere few fragments of whatever had been left out. Rats were disgusting, but she decided that snakes were much worse. They were dangerous.

Andi admitted that one good thing had come out of her close encounter with the brown snake on the verandah: Daisy seemed more willing to get involved with the house. Although even *that* seemed a barbed blessing, because everything Daisy did, had attitude, as if she was out to prove a point. Andi was not brave enough to tell her that she didn't know anyone who really cared what her point was. Still, the verandah was cleaned up, and they started on the bedrooms. Finally, Andi could say with confidence that they were working towards their part of the rental agreement.

Every so often, they would open the front door in the morning to find something left on the verandah. Usually there was a billy of fresh milk. Once there was a new bucket and mop. Well – it wasn't shop-new. The bucket was made from an old square kerosene tin with the top edge beaten over, and a twisted wire handle. But there were no holes in it and Andi appreciated that more than the others because it meant less trips to the tank. The mop was made from strips of old rag, bunched together and bound with fencing wire to the end of a handle. They figured it was Harry's doing, but he never admitted it.

Another morning, there was a big bundle of used curtains and sheets by the door. That day had been like Christmas. They spent the day in a frenzy of redecorating… hanging 'new' curtains that were already faded and worn with the occasional neatly sewn patch. They were much better than the bare windows. Some of the old sheets were put aside to recover the lounge. Daisy even tucked some away for her private use. They salvaged what they could from the tatted old curtains for making rag-mats and cleaning rags, and the rest joined the growing pile of rubbish over the fence. They scrubbed walls and windows and floors and worked well past the afternoon curfew. Now the lounge room was well on the way to being respectable too.

They often saw Harry working on the block next

door. There were stacks of hand-hewn timber and large beams, that he brought in with his Clydesdale draught horse, its large hairy hooves dragging under the weight of his load. One morning Jo and Andi were dumping a box full of stuff over the fence, when he called to them. "Hey! Want to see something?"

Curiously they went over to where Harry had pegged out a large square area and was digging holes along its perimeter. He loosened dirt in the hole with a crowbar and then stabbed it into the ground, so it stood by itself like a thin iron sapling. He shovelled out the loose dirt into a pile. "Over here…." he said, taking the shovel with him. It was wise to always have a snake weapon, just in case. It never used to be like this… the prickly pear provided an unnatural haven where normal predators could not reach. When one thing gets out of balance, a whole stack of other problems come with it. In their case – a population explosion of snakes… death adders mostly. Harry pointed to a huge clump of prickly pear. "Take a look at that..." he said, almost bashfully.

Jo looked bewildered at the monotonous green mass before her. And there tucked in the base was the modestly decorated bower of a bower bird. "Oh wow! Even in a prickly pear patch some little bird can make an interesting little home." She shook her head in fascination.

"He hasn't got much to work with here, but he still gave it a go. Kinda thought that was an idea worth noticing." Harry smiled. "But it was not so much this that I wanted to show you. I have never seen anything more beautiful in my life, than this particular patch of pear..." he said with uncharacteristic enthusiasm.

Jo searched to see if there was something else other than the abandoned bowerbird's construction. Nothing looked special. In the stillness of the hot late morning sun not even a breeze stirred. "I can't see anything else. No birds, no rabbits, no bugs... nothing!" she announced.

Andi peered in through the tangled mass. Everything looked the Same... *except... maybe...* "I know!" she said jumping straight up. "I know, I know, I know!"

Jo narrowed her eyes and looked intensely. She hated being out done. "There is nothing else there."

Andi raised her eyebrows mysteriously. "Oh, but there is…"

"Rot! You're just saying that."

"Exactly!" said Andi triumphantly. "It's *rot*! Real rot. That's it – isn't it, Harry? The leaves are turning. Over there they are sort of hollow and yellow and collapsing. It's starting to die!"

Jo looked at the clump again. Evidence that it was being attacked from the inside becoming clearer. "Wow.

Does this mean the plague is over?"

Harry laughed. He hadn't felt this good in a long time. The suit-men were right! It was working, and he didn't have to *do* anything – except believe them and follow their simple instructions. It was almost too simple. No wonder everyone had a healthy dose of scepticism. "Well," he said honestly, "I want to believe it's the start of fixing our problems… and it looks kinda hopeful. This is the sickest pest-pear I've ever seen... and I've seen plenty!"

"How did you find a poison that finally works on it?" asked Andi. She had heard the stories of the battle against this indestructible pest.

"It's not poison, but a moth from Argentina called the Cactoblastis. The grubs only eat prickly pear. The Prickly Pear Commission provided straws with the eggs of the moth in 'em a couple of months back – we just had to stab them into the leaves."

"That's it?" Just then she spotted an orange little grub burrow it's way over a spongy leaf.

"Yep. I jabbed this clump – because it was the biggest. I figured this would be a fair test to see if it this Cactoblastis could make a difference."

"Blastus-the-cactus!" exclaimed Jo. "How do you get more straws? Is it ever going to spread far enough to get rid of it all?"

"I've checked other areas where I used the quills on Dad and Mum's place. It seemed like nothing was happening for a long time, but they are all looking very much like this one now. Those little grubs won't die of starvation that's for certain – there's plenty of food. My guess is if the reign of Prickly Pear isn't over... it is at least under serious threat."

For the next few weeks, they watched with fascination, as cactus yellowed and blackened; becoming sicker and sicker. Neighbours came to watch the rot set in, in the wake of the hungry grubs eating frenzy. That condemned patch of pear was eaten from the inside out. Jo and Andi used some hessian bags to protect their hands from the spines and borrowed some infested leaves where they could see the orange and black grubs enthusiastically eating their way to adulthood. They strategically placed them around their house-yard in the hope that the larvae would burrow their way into their personal collection of thriving domesticated prickly pear plants... and then the adult moths might lay eggs there as well, and the cycle continue.

The girls planned that as soon as there was some space, they were going to dig a garden. They'd found some seeds in an old tin in the cupboard. Each envelope was labelled in scratchy handwriting: tomatoes, pumpkin, daisies, marrow and sweet-peas. Jo was very dubious they'd grow... but she figured if nothing else, they could serve as compost. At least they had been protected from becoming rat food. That alone, meant they deserved the chance to be planted in a garden bed.

* * *

There is something about construction that inspires a community. Harry's shed became such a symbol to Gum Ridge. He didn't have the benefit of the instant "barn-raisings" famous in the American West where whole communities would up tools for a two-day working-bee. Harry's shed was his project, and the locals respected that. But that didn't stop them watching with interest as it was being erected. He mostly worked on it himself, the neighbours dropping past to have smoko of billy-tea, fresh scones and prickly-pear jam which Margaret had put in his basket that morning. They'd check out how it was going and talked with droll humour about the progress of the cactoblastis miracle.

More farmers who had not followed through on the quills came and inspected Harry's dying pear-patch with great interest. As the cycle of the Moth progressed and new eggs were laid, they would carefully cradle some of the tiny threadlike white egg-sticks home and gently nurture their existence with the protective care of a mother hen. Each little stick hatched forty or so tiny grubs that would work together to gnaw through the tough skin of the cactus... and then disperse to get on with the business of growing. This was a reason to celebrate and suddenly this community was not just nurturing grubs... it was nurturing the hope that their ambitions of survival were not in vain. Slowly the plans for their farms and their families, which had long been buried in the harsh reality of the plague, began to germinate again.

Over their mug of billy-tea they would talk about these invigorated dreams. They'd chat while they gave a hand to lift heavy beams of the shed's frame into place. Harry never had to canvas for help because everyone knew exactly what stage the shed was at. If he needed a hand, there was always someone close by.

Jo and Andi spent a lot of their afternoons over the fence with Harry, holding timber, passing hammers and nails, brace and bits, pliers and wire. It was much more interesting than spending the afternoon skirting around Daisy's snide comments and bitter interjections.

When they were gone, Daisy would go behind the lounge chair and dig out some fabric she had saved from the bundle of curtains. She laid it out carefully on the table and trimmed and cut shapes out with an old razor blade. Sometimes she got very little done on her secret project before the girls came bounding up the old wooden verandah steps. She always tried to do something towards this project each day. Even a small line of simple hand sewing using a rather rusty needle and thread she had pulled from some old sheeting. She became totally absorbed. She would be rude and abrupt so Andi and Jo would leave the house early to help Harry just to escape. That way she had more time to herself, and she could work on her project undisturbed.

The agitation made Jo and Andi want to leave Gum Ridge with greater urgency. If Daisy had been some sort of saint, Andi felt she could patiently endure the suffering like a persecuted martyr. But Daisy was as enthusiastic for their company as snuggling down with an echidna. And still the residents of Gum Ridge ostracised them so they inhabited their own personal leper-colony of three. "We should walk around with a bell and a sign that says: 'Unclean! Danger! Residing with Daisy! Unclean!'" said Jo in disgust one morning as they walked through town and watched as people crossed the street to avoid them. They were given dark looks and a wide berth by everyone they saw. Jo felt a particular pang when the little girl with light curls – Ruby, her father had called her, was quickly bundled out of their way as if the very sight of them would cause collapse from a deadly disease.

It all seemed really pointless. Andi insisted that if

Daisy was the reason for them coming to Gum Ridge, then they had to believe that somehow staying and hanging around would make a difference. But that one simple thing was not simple. Even Andi admitted sometimes it just seemed too hard. "Bless her, Jesus," she would pray through gritted teeth. "Bless her, because to bless her you will have to change a whole stack of things."

Helping Harry on his building project was their one place of relief in life at Gum Ridge. He was never rude... but listened with a silent smile as they prattled about their renovation projects and frustrations with Daisy. Harry never said a bad thing about Daisy, and when they got particularly verbal, he would just sigh and say, "You are doing okay. She needs a friend. Hang in there."

At times they would find things suddenly fixed, like the door on the out-house. It had dangled precariously on its broken hinge, and their attempt to mend it had just ended in it being utterly broken. The entire passing traffic on the road was exposed to their private happenings whenever they had to visit the outside toilet even if it was out the back of the yard. They would schedule their visits together so one person could prop the door up against the gapping entrance, and then lift it out of the way when they were finished. Daisy was completely unperturbed. She banged in a couple of nails and slung an old curtain across the doorway, but the girls didn't like the way it flapped in the wind. It was totally humiliating. Curiously within the next few days, a new toilet door appeared swinging like a dream on new black-smithed hinges. They made Harry a cake for that, but the seal on the oven door was shot, so it didn't work out very well. It sort of flopped in the middle and tasted rather sooty. Harry ate it like it was his Ma's favourite recipe.

The shed slowly took shape. Even before the roof was finished, Doctor Arthur Larsen brought his car over for advice from Harry to find out why it wasn't running smoothly. Harry talked to him about regular services and organised times when he could work on the car when he was not visiting patients. Anyway, Doctor Larsen still had to use his horse on most of the roads because they were impassable to his motorised car.

Late one afternoon Mr and Mrs Telford brought their new machine over to show Harry their investment with pride. He went over the car inch by inch, telling them all the wonderful features of this new model, so that they flushed with excitement. As they were leaving, he crank-started it for them and said he would order in the special oil they needed. They waved enthusiastically as they chugged off in a cloud of dust.

The girls were fascinated that everyone seemed to

like Harry. No one ever doubted his sincerity, and they never had reason to. Everyone that is, except Daisy. When Harry came over one morning with an invitation from his mother to join them for Sunday lunch after Church, she flatly refused to go. But there was no way Andi and Jo were going to be left fending for themselves when there was the prospect of a real farm-kitchen baked dinner on the menu. They wrote out a polite acceptance and gave apologies on behalf of Daisy. Sunday couldn't come quick enough.

* * *

9

Mr and Mrs Dunn were going to come by and pick up the girls before church. "They probably think they are going to covert us," said Jo with a smirk as she slipped on her shoes.

"Then they'll be disappointed – it's already done," said Andi shuffling into the dress and beads she had worn to that first theatre outing. "Still – it is nice they think we are worth the effort. No one else does."

There was a firm rap on the door. Mr Dunn helped the girls climb into the sulky, while saying their greetings and introductions. Mrs Dunn looked disapprovingly at Andi's beads. The plain dress that Margaret wore was old-fashioned and long. It was evidently her Sunday best, and it would have been improved greatly by some simple beads, thought Andi when she saw her grimace.

"Where's Harry?" asked Jo innocently enjoying the prospect of an outing.

His mother looked even grimmer. "He is *greeting* this morning, handing out the hymn books," said Mrs Dunn firmly.

Mr Dunn flicked the reigns and added amiably. "It's easier for him to make his own way to church. Then he can stay and catch up afterwards if he wants."

"Oh," mumbled Jo with a smile towards his father. It was obvious where Harry got his easy-going ways from. Mrs Dunn on the other hand, looked like she was suffering a bilious attack from having eaten too much prickly pear with the prickles still attached. Jo had kind of expected that this family would be different. But it seemed their joke about their conversion candidacy, was no joke at all. Mrs Dunn *was* doing her Christian duty and trying to save them from whatever it was she thought they needed saving from. Too bad her missionary zeal was in vain.

"I want to thank you for your kind invitation Mrs Dunn," said Andi in an attempt to lighten the frosty atmosphere.

"You're welcome," she said icily. "It is our duty to get to know the tenants…."

"Duty?" choked Jo. Andi quickly jabbed her in the ribs so that Jo started coughing. Whatever did Mrs Dunn mean?

"I trust the arrangements that Harry has made with you as tenants are suitable," Mrs Dunn continued grimly.

"Harry? Yesss…" Andi hesitated. "I understood this invitation was a social outing – not a business one."

Mr Dunn quietly smiled… and Mrs Dunn cleared her throat. "Yes of course – but it is best to get it all out in the open. We are aware the house is less than perfect..." Jo started coughing again. "... but being there on a charity basis should..."

So! The derelict house belonged to the Dunns. If Harry owned the house with his parents, the charitable agreement with Daisy did not surprise her at all. That's something Harry would do... but in a way Andi felt a bit disappointed. It explained why he was so willing to help out. He wasn't just being neighbourly because he considered them friends; he was looking after his investment.

"Now Margaret, I'm sure the girls will let us know if there are any problems with the house. They don't look the kind to blab to uninvolved parties."

That hardly seemed a relevant concern; no one ever talked to them anyway. Andi smiled at the way Mr Dunn affirmed his confidence in them. Mrs Dunn was obviously worried about what people would think if they complained about the state of the house. Yet, if Mrs Dunn was so concerned about what the locals would think, why would she agree to them being in the house at all? Having Daisy Brown and associates as tenants was not the way to win a popularity contest in Gum Ridge.

The thin horse pulled into the grounds of the little weatherboard church. The girls took Mr Dunn's hand and stepped down into the dust. They felt the looks and comments behind gloved hands directed their way. Jo resolutely raised her head and took Andi by the arm. "Chin up Andi. This is God's meeting place… surely we'll be allowed a little slack here."

Harry met them at the door and handed them a large navy hymnbook to share. He shook their hand formally and smiled reassuringly. Jo looked at the stark wooden pews. *If comfort is a pagan trait, these people are saints,* thought Jo as she sat stiffly on a hard bench. A large middle-aged woman sat pumping a pedal organ. A pulpit was featured front and centre, and a man in black robes sat on a chair behind it, his head bowed.

Andi and Jo sat with Mrs and Mr Dunn as murmuring rippled through the gathering. A couple of girls started giggling behind their hands. Andi squirmed uncomfortably. Jo looked around and spotted Ruby. Her red-headed doll had on its best Sunday hat and sat demurely in her lap.

Jo waved a finger 'hello' and Ruby smiled; the kind of smile that lights up a room. Her little fingers quietly took her doll's arm and it gave a wave in return. Her mother was whispering something behind her hand to her husband.

Just then a poker-faced woman stood up in the front row. She looked as if she'd been in a pear sucking competition with Mrs Dunn and had quite clearly won. She glared at Jo and Andi, and noisily collected her things. The woman adjusted her sleeves and hat, lifted her chin and jabbed the man beside her. He stood up and she took his arm. Jo raised her eyebrows as she recognised him as the man from the hotel. They paused and looked significantly at Ruby's parents. "Come Gladys, no daughter of mine is going to suffer this indignity!" muttered the woman clearly enough for everyone to hear. Gladys hurriedly gathered their things and walked back out of the church with the pear-sucking woman, pulling Ruby behind them. Sid from the Post Office followed the hotel man outside.

Mrs Dunn's face flushed bright red, and she patted her forehead with a worn lace-trimmed handkerchief. Jo turned around and watched them leave. As they got to the door, Ruby held out her arms and gave Harry a huge hug. He quickly dug in his pockets and pulled out a little polished stone and tucked it in her hand. She carefully wrapped it in her handkerchief and stuffed it in the pocket of her pinafore. It was obviously not the first time Harry had some treasure to give to her. They left then in a hurry.

The parson lifted his eyes and watched this protest in silence. He studied Jo and Andi quietly. He knew what the parishioners were saying. He sighed. There was no accounting for small town politics sometimes.

He rose, his robes rustling on the timber floor as he made a call to worship and announced the first hymn. The organ wheezed out an opening chord, and the congregation struggled to its feet. Their voices strained to hit the high notes and the music got slower and slower as the organist laboriously pedalled wind through the bellows. The lady behind them screeched loudly and the tone had the same effect on Andi as someone running their finger nails down a chalk-board. By the time they had agonized their way through three verses Jo was ready to climb under the benches and commando-crawl her way out of the torture-chamber.

They finished the hymn and the congregation sat noisily. One of the kids bumped his mother's handbag and it crashed loudly on the floor, spewing its contents under the next three rows. There was a scramble to pick up the debris, while the rest of the congregation settled with more banging and scraping, books dropping on the wooden floor. "Beloved let us love one another, for love is from God...let us pray..." and he embarked on a prayer of confession and intercession.

Jo bowed her head and at the same time tried to look around to see if she recognised anyone. No one seemed to be listening. She saw ladies adjusting their gloves, fathers slapping fidgeting children, kids picking their noses and boys racing beetles along the back of the pews. One of the lads was so engrossed in the beetle sprint, that he let out a victorious "Yes!" as his bug crossed the finishing groove in the bench. The minister raised his closed eyes to the ceiling believing it to be encouragement to pray harder and longer. Jo jabbed Andi in the ribs and nodded towards one man who was dozing off. He sat propped up against the wall, his eyes half open showing the whites of his eyes. He sort-of snorted through his nose as his head and shoulders relaxed and he startled himself upright once more. The minister kept going… and going… and going. When he launched into praying for African pagans Andi felt herself inwardly groan. Sure, she wanted everyone to know and love God, but she didn't think it absolutely necessary to mention them all now! Finally, he closed, and a gentleman at the back gave a resounding "Amen!"

Andi had never been so bored in her life. She wondered why people would go to church and suffer through this. "Oh gee, Jesus – I hope you're enjoying this, because nobody else seems to be!" All her energy went into sitting still and trying not to embarrass Mr and Mrs Dunn for bringing them. She didn't want to miss their one and only invitation to Sunday dinner.

Finally, the sermon finished and they rose for the concluding hymn. The promise of dinner coming closer made Jo's tummy rumble noisily. Mrs Dunn glanced sideways in disapproval. "Excuse me," mumbled Jo, but it didn't dampen the volume of the stomach rumbles so she had to develop a serious coughing disorder to cover the noise. It was not like she was doing it intentionally. Finally, they sang a closing benediction and the girls waited as people systematically filed out of the church shaking the minister's hand with gushing accolades about how his long-winded sermon was *such a blessing*.

"They've got to be kidding!" thought Jo, "How can they say that with a straight face? Any one in their right mind would have to admit it was physical and mental torture!" Jo was not even sure the endurance-event was worth a Sunday dinner invitation. She just hoped the food was pretty good.

Somehow, they were the last to leave the church. Harry was stacking hymnbooks in wooden boxes into a cupboard out the back. The minister had already made his way down to the front packing his things up. The girls glanced out the door and saw Mr and Mrs Dunn making small talk with the neighbours. They didn't want to go out there. Everywhere they went people fell silent as they walked past. "Need some help with those books Harry?" they volunteered.

"Sure. Stick 'em in there," he said and went down

the front to shake the minister's hand. Harry helped him pack up. The minister had shed his robes. Underneath he had an ordinary brown suit that was carefully patched in a couple of places. He paused and quietly leaned on the pulpit.

"Harry," he said, "I don't think I'm reaching these people. You're the only one I ever seem to make a connection with. Why is that? What am I doing here? Have I missed God's calling?"

Harry looked thoughtful and smiled at him. "Sir, you've got more heart for these folks than any I know. I don't doubt God will use that to minister to them."

"But Harry. You see 'em every Sunday I come through. Without exception they'd rather be somewhere else. Why they keep coming beats me."

"Well Reverend, it maybe they know God can meet their needs where no one else can."

"Or they feel that God will beat them up if they don't show. How can I get them to understand God *loves* them? I talk 'til I'm blue in the face. They just aren't getting it."

"Perhaps that's it Reverend."

"What is?"

"These people have it tough. It's been that way for a long, long time. They have dry and hungry spirits. We only have church every few weeks because of your circuit."

He cleared his throat. "Maybe it's too much..." he suggested tentatively.

The man looked startled. And then he laughed. "Well, I'll be blowed! I think you're right. That's it isn't it?" He thumped Harry on the back good naturedly. He paused and shook his head. "I feel that my work should make a difference but it just doesn't seem to. I reckon it could really be too much, too soon. That's just what Saint Peter talked about – giving milk to babies and working up to a solid diet!" He pumped Harry's hand. "Bless you brother. I have more hope in five minutes than I have had all year. Bless you," he repeated enthusiastically. "God's not finished with me yet."

Harry smiled. "'Nor me. Never thought for a moment he might be," he said as he picked up the saddlebags and carried them to the door and went out to get the parson's horse tethered in the paddock next door. "We'll see you next time then."

"God willing, should the good Lord tarry." He stopped as he passed the girls sitting by the box of hymnbooks. As he looked into their faces, he could not bring himself to believe the gossipy words he had heard bandied around. Besides, Mrs Dunn was not one to be led astray by immoral company. He wanted to offer them a word of encouragement – but nothing came to mind. He stuck out his hand instead. "It was a pleasure to have some fresh faces with us this morning," he said sincerely.

Jo could hardly contain the grunt that sat under her diaphragm like an irrepressible belch. Andi took his offered hand and shook it. "We appreciate that. It seems not everyone is so enthusiastic about us being here."

Once he would have tried to deny it heartily, but Harry's example of honesty – even in its awkwardness, was fresh in his mind. Harry had not just spoken the truth, but he had said it out of concern and love for him as a friend. The sad reality was, these two young ladies were not welcome. It was only because the Dunn family had a long and honoured place in the community that they could survive any connection with these girls at all. He nodded, acknowledging the truth of what Andi had said. He smiled sadly. "I know. I feel embarrassed that those Jesus would have welcomed are made to feel like outcasts."

Jo sat up straight. "And what does *that* mean? *Who* would Jesus have welcomed? You make us sound like Pharisees, or tax-collectors… or prostitutes!" Jo was needled by being the brunt of bad manners all the time. They had done nothing wrong. They didn't just *feel* like outcasts – they were!

The minister coughed and flushed with embarrassment at the challenge. "Now, now," he murmured, "Jesus welcomes us all… children and adults alike. All have sinned and fallen short of the glory of God."

"That's not what you meant at all," said Jo defensively. "You believe all the lies they have been telling each other. The only difference being that because you wear religious garb, you're supposed to be above it. You are no better than the rest of them!"

"Jo!" hissed Andi in embarrassment. "Keep it down."

"Why? They all think that because we live with Daisy, we must be morally impaired. Well I'm sick of it. It wasn't our choice."

Now he felt completely at sea. He was not used to people, even young people, challenging his discernment. His ears were protected. Around a minister, people carefully chose their words, and changed their speech like their Sunday shirts. He looked like a rabbit stunned by a pellet gun as Jo stood beside the hymn book boxes her eyes flashing with hurt and defiance, daring him to prove her wrong. But he couldn't.

"Dear Lord," he prayed silently, *"What is with all this honesty? Show me how to love in truth."* God must have delighted in such a prayer because the sting of her insolence faded, and the hurt in her eyes became more visible. He suddenly felt protective, like a father towards his daughter,

or a shepherd towards his sheep. In a flash of insight, he understood more of what a pastor needed to be. People may not hear words, but they will hear care and kindness. "I'm sorry. I made a judgement, forgive me…" He would have said more but Mrs Dunn bundled through the door.

"Reverend would you care to join us for Sunday dinner? It is a long ride to your next church and I…. Unless you have a prior engagement of course." Margaret knew full well he had no other invitations. The parishioners will punish him because he didn't make a stand against the girls.

"Mrs Dunn. Thank you. I would be delighted." He was relieved. He had run out of the food his gentle young wife had packed for him. Sometimes the itinerant life was more a burden than a privilege.

* * *

They sat out on the verandah sipping flat orangeade while Mrs Dunn busied herself in the kitchen. Roast smells wafted through the house. Mr Dunn and Harry talked parish business with Reverend McKinley while the girls hungrily tried to be patient. Eventually they were ushered into the dining room. Andi felt they were entering a holy place. The linen tablecloth was starched and crisp, the table set with their best china, the chips on the rims turned to disguise their battle-weary edges.

They sat down and Mr Dunn asked the minister to

give thanks for the meal. Every one bowed their head. Jo's mouth watered as she looked at the serving platter set in the centre of the table and wondered if they would *ever* get to eat. Asking this man to pray was asking for a long dissertation on every virtue and characteristic of God… and that was before he even started on their own flawed human state. "Oh Lord our heavenly Father…" he began. Jo groaned before she realised, she had done it out loud. She quickly cleared her throat in embarrassment. "…we thank you for your bountiful provision and grace…" He paused to take a deep breath and Andi could tell he was winding up for a really long prayer. She opened her eye just a slit and tantalised her taste buds. The lean roast chicken was sitting, all angles, on the Sunday platter in the centre of the table. To Jo it was a vision of succulent, plump and crispy bliss. Reverend McKinley hesitated and then quickly said "…bless this generous family and their friends…Amen."

"Amen," echoed the others in amazement.

Mrs Dunn looked quite disappointed. "That was a very brief prayer, Reverend McKinley," she lamented.

"Your excellent cooking, Mrs Dunn, is none less appreciated because I was briefer than usual in giving my thanks to God. I believe our heavenly Father understands cooking such as yours speaks for itself," and he flicked his worn serviette, starched and ironed, onto his lap. Mrs Dunn looked unsure but she passed the roast chicken to the head of the table. Mr Dunn picked up his knife and started to carve it. Then the food was passed around.

Jo and Andi tucked in. Their wait was well worth it. For Sunday lunch - with guests, Mrs Dunn splurged on a chicken from the hen house with gravy and roast vegetables that she nurtured in her house garden. Granted they were roasted chokos, turnips and sweet potatoes – hardy things that could grow under concrete, and spinach that is a tough farmhouse constant. In more lush times Margaret would have discarded spinach in favour of tender climbing beans… but that hadn't been possible for seasons now. For dessert there was not a Prickly Pear fruit anywhere to be seen. Instead, they had apple and rhubarb pie with lashings of thin egg custard.

The apple pie was a mystery to Andi – she had not noticed apples for sale in any of the shops. She hesitantly offered her admiration of Mrs Dunn's abilities. Margaret looked at Andi carefully and asked if she would help her clear the dishes. As they took them out to the kitchen Mrs Dunn whispered, "I don't like to talk domestics in front of the men. They don't understand…"

Jo was following behind. "Perhaps if we did – they would get to understand," she said.

"Not likely dear," followed Mrs Dunn quite serenely.

"It is far too complex." Jo laughed outright at that. It was the last thing she expected Mrs Dunn to say. Margaret turned around and relaxed a little. These girls were not at all what she had expected.

Andi had to ask. "The apple pie was amazing – but I've never even seen a fresh apple in Gum Ridge."

"Fresh apples - at this time of year dear? Never. But apple pie never goes out of season. Men like their pie."

"So how do you do it?" Andi asked curiously. Lack of deep freezers and pre-cooked brand cakes naturally implied that certain things could not be readily available, no matter how much you liked your pie!

"I always preserve a few apples when they are brought in on the train. To bake the pie, I use just the smallest jar, and bulk it out with rhubarb and chokos. A touch of sugar and no one can ever tell the difference."

Andi raised her eyebrows in amazement. She had expected Mrs Dunn to carefully guard her culinary secrets. "Wow. Could you teach me to do that? What we eat is so disgusting. Daisy might be clever at some things – but cooking is not one of them!"

The mention of Daisy brought Mrs Dunn back to earth with a thud. She stared at them both. "I hope you girls know what you're doing, being with her," Mrs Dunn said soberly.

Jo didn't like the way this always came up; but it did. They could never just be themselves – they were always Daisy's attachments. At the moment they were in survival mode. "Andi's right – she's a lousy cook. Your cooking is the best," she said.

Mrs Dunn paused. It wouldn't hurt to pass on something the years had taught her. It was not like she had a daughter to teach. She hesitated. "Cooking is just the last phase in a long process of preparation. There's more than I can show you in an afternoon."

"It's not like we've got a lot on our calendar at the moment…"

It was unusual – that they would not have learnt these things from their own mothers. The thought they might be motherless victims of fate, softened Margaret's opinion of their association with Daisy. "I'll get Harry to bring you over a couple of days a week. He's back and forwards a bit now that he finished the shed and taking the tools down into his workshop. Then we can go over some things… kitchen and the garden… it all goes hand in hand."

It was settled. They had embarked on a farmhouse cooking apprenticeship with the master of all local cooks.

* * *

10

One day they were helping Mrs Dunn gather the ingredients to make paddymelon and prickly pear jam. Jo looked very dubious as they piled the wild bush melons on the bench. They looked like stunted rock melons without the flavour or texture of any real melon she had ever experienced. They prepared the prickly pear fruit by rubbing the fruit around in a hessian bag to brush off the prickles and washing them carefully.

"Are you sure the jam will taste okay putting these things into it?" Andi asked hesitantly. "This doesn't look like it's going to have much flavour."

Margaret could not get used to these girls' very peculiar ideas about food. She was sure it was because of the sheltered, inflexible ways of the city where they had obviously met up with Daisy. They just had no idea about basic domestic skills, but she conceded at least they were willing to give it a try. She just wished they didn't have to analyse everything. That was not the way she had learnt.

Her childhood had been characterised by listening and taking it in – absorption method. Questions were a sign of sassiness. It took every ounce of her concentration to stay composed. "You had it on your damper for morning tea. I believe you thought it was tasty then," she reminded them.

"That jam was *this* recipe?"

Margaret nodded and set them to work peeling and scraping and chopping. "Eewh! This is so disgusting. I can't imagine this muck in my mouth!" said Jo as she chopped into yet another unappetising melon.

Margaret relieved Jo of chopping the fruit by sending her out to get some wood from the wood-box. Finally, they were able to set the boiler on the stove, stirring with the wooden spoon and watching the sugar dissolve. Then they began the ritual of scalding jars in boiling water, fixing labels with today's date and preparing paraffin wax to seal the top of the jars.

"Why don't you just use bottles with lids?" asked Andi.

There was constantly another question they had to ask. Why couldn't they just accept there was always a reason... and usually a very good one. "These jars are cut down from old bottles. That way I can have as many as I need and can make them as tall or as low as I like," said Mrs Dunn pointing to her pantry store. Andi peered into the little room where rows of preserves and jams were lined up like uniformed soldiers, according to size. Harry had created a whole new set for her birthday one year, using a metal ring on tongs in his forge to slip over the bottle to create the exact same height for the jars.

Mrs Dunn tested the jam on a saucer, waiting for the juice to wrinkle in a particular way as it cooled. Soon they were in a frenzy of bottling and sealing. It was a fiddly process. Jo decided grocery shopping was not such a terrible chore after all. It beats having to spend the entire day in a sweltering kitchen hovering over a wood stove, just to get jam for your morning toast. Finally, they finished the cleaning up. Jam making is a messy job.

Mrs Dunn brought their lunch out to the verandah that overlooked the farm. It was complete with pikelets so they could taste their very own jam – still warm from the pot. Andi swallowed a mouth full of pikelet and turned to Mrs Dunn. "We have nearly finished fixing up the house – well, as much as we can do without major renovations. We wanted to celebrate – with a dinner, and we would like you and Mr Dunn to come along, and Harry of course. I don't think anyone else would come, even if we invited them."

Margaret Dunn looked thoughtfully out over the paddocks. For once she didn't say anything about Daisy. "It would be our pleasure to accept," she said. Margaret realised having these two in her kitchen encouraged her in ways she had not expected. Once Harry walked past the table as they were in the middle of a lesson on kneading bread. He had a look of complete amazement on his face. He had never seen anyone in his mother's kitchen before. Yes, these cooking lessons had been a good idea.

"How about you girls come over before you start preparing your dinner and help yourselves to the pantry. It's the least I could do since you've been working hard on your visits here." Margaret patted her stove-flushed face and drank her watery cup of tea. She sat stiffly as they both squealed in delight and flung themselves over her in a hug. She smiled quietly and awkwardly patted their back. *Yes, learning at her age was hard work, but well worth it. She must never be too old to learn.*

* * *

Daisy didn't involve herself too much in what the girls did. A shrug and a sigh was usually as much as they had come to expect from her when they told her anything. However, when they mentioned about the dinner invitation, they had extended to the Dunn family, she went ballistic. She *really* went off. She stormed around the house reminding them of every bad experience they had since coming to Gum Ridge. "And to top it off," she screamed, "you want to invite some of them here! Here! How could you? We've finally settled. This is the one place where we don't have to look at these hypocrites and listen to their comments!"

Jo starred at her in amazement. "Oh, give me a break. You know Harry. He's not like that; anyway, he's been here plenty of times. His parents are okay. Besides *we* live here too, and *we* want to have company. You could go out for the night."

"Sure – where to? I'm certainly not going to roam the streets."

"Well, stay in your room then!" Jo flung back at her.

Andi tried to calmly restore peace. "Jo – that's not fair. Daisy lives here as well."

"Exactly! She seems to forget that also means *we* live here. Why does everything have to orbit around Planet Daisy?" said Jo testily.

"Daisy – why is it so terrible we want to say thank you? They are the only people who've made an effort to be nice to us. If it wasn't for them, we'd have nowhere to stay. Surely we could…"

"What do you mean?" Daisy said quickly.

"Well, you know – since they're our landlords. Harry could throw us out as quick as look at us, but he's stuck his head out letting us stay here… and he's always fixing things. None of the other locals would do it and you know it. We just want to celebrate finishing the house… and sort of thank them at the same time."

Daisy went quite pale and sat down. "Harry Dunn?"

she whispered.

"Yeah – and his parents, no one else. Just a small dinner. We thought next Sunday after Church. You could come with us to the service…" Andi tentatively floated the idea of getting her out of the house for an outing. Daisy never went anywhere. Andi seemed to have suffered temporary amnesia about being so bored during the church service she thought she'd asphyxiate.

"No way. Nope – nothing doing. You'll have to cancel."

Jo rolled her eyes. "Daisy this is *real* food we are talking here. Mrs Dunn has given us free reign of her pantry. You've never seen a pantry like it! There is no way I am going to cancel!"

Daisy paused and looked at Jo. "Mrs Dunn – that is, Mrs *Margaret* Dunn, let you look inside her pantry?"

"Not only that," countered Jo, "But she said we can take whatever we need to help prepare our dinner. Come on – you *have* to agree… it won't work if you go all snooty on us."

"Well thanks for the vote of confidence. I can be a delightful hostess given the occasion," said Daisy with a little pout, thinking of her cocktail parties she had staged in the city.

Andi relaxed and took that to mean she would be

fully cooperative. "Great! No problem then," and she launched into menu ideas she thought would be a hospitable change from bread and dripping.

"But…" Daisy started to object; however, she could see on this occasion she was seriously out-voted. These girls knew nothing about how to host an event. Perhaps if she helped them, she could get away with minimal disruption and embarrassment. Not likely though.

Harry was sure to raise the fact she had set herself up on his property without permission. Daisy sighed. She was so proud this house was the one thing that had gone well for her. Until now she had no idea who was the owner. The only information Daisy had been able to find out about the house was that it was vacant, and it was expected to stay that way forever because of its state of disrepair. No one was forth coming about who owned it – because that information would imply the locals at Gum Ridge approved of her staying. Daisy's concocted story about cleaning it up in lieu of rent was intended to minimise the fuss the girls would make about squatting on someone else's land illegally.

Daisy had been irritated by Harry's persistent neighbourliness. She tolerated it because she figured he would be less likely to say anything around town if he didn't suspect anything was improper. She went over in her mind every time he had come to fix things. He emptied the rat-trap every morning, and even spent an entire afternoon cleaning out the fire place chimney in the lounge room. They were no longer smoked out when they lit the fire on cool evenings. Harry had gone home looking like a black and white minstrel there had been so much soot. Yet in all that time he never even hinted he owned the house or that he was anything other than a friendly neighbour. Why didn't he say something? The more Daisy thought about it the more she became convinced that this dinner would have to dazzle him into leaving them alone in his house.

* * *

Mr Dunn looked appreciatively at the empty plates as Andi gathered them up. "Ladies, that meal was first-rate. Thank you." Andi beamed radiantly. A simple comment like that made every ounce of trauma the preparation of their Sunday lunch had caused, worthwhile.

The stove was the major problem. Cooking was an adventure in pyrotechnics. There was a dark charred patch on the wall where they nearly burnt down the house during one of their practice runs. Harry was working on his shed next door and had responded to their screams. He beat out the fire and then came back the next day and cleaned out a rat's nest from inside the flue. He hammered up some metal sheets around the stove as a fire shield and did some work on the firebox. But they knew with this oven, they would never turn out the beautifully cooked delicacies his mother could, but at least with practise the food was edible.

Margaret had grudgingly approved of the effort they had gone to. The potato was sloshy and the pumpkin had hard bony bits that put her teeth on edge. She didn't like the way it was presented in fancy little swirls with fiddly little bits of garnish hanging off everywhere. Still, she restrained herself and made no comments about the obvious flaws in their cooking and ate in silence. Dessert had been okay as well... an apple crumble featuring some of her apple preserves and a sprinkling of cinnamon sugar.

Daisy poured out a cup of tea and passed around some short-bread that was hard and crunchy. Harry smiled his thanks. "You know. This is a double celebration. Your house and my shed." Daisy tried not to wince as he said, "your house". Harry continued. "I've moved all the tools down here now. I've fixed my bellows and with the forge I'll be able take blacksmithing jobs again until more mechanical work comes in. We are ready to open for business!"

Andi and Jo burst out into unrestrained applause and Andi stood earnestly as they were finishing their cup of tea. "Thank you so much for coming. There is one more thing we want to do before you go. Our pile of the rubbish from our clean-up is ready as a bon-fire to mark the occasion. Mr Dunn – would you do the honours and start the fire for us?"

Mr Dunn was always the gentleman. He went right along with the girls' quirky little ceremony and didn't complain that he had on his best Sunday clothes. He just rolled his shirt-sleeves up out of the way. He collected some coals from the kitchen stove putting them in the bottom of their leaky tin bucket and carried them out to the heap.

The whole thing was frivolous to Margaret. Fair enough they wanted to burn their rubbish-heap... but why make it into some sort of ritual? "You girls go and watch your ceremonial burning; I'll do the washing up. It's the least I can do for your hospitality," she said when the girls urged her to come and watch.

"But Mrs Dunn – we really wanted you not to do any work today. It is your day off," objected Andi.

"Women never have days off, Sabbath or not. You go ahead now – or you'll miss your fiery spectacular," she said briskly.

Andi complied and went outside. If anyone else had offered to do the washing up – it would have been a generous offer, but somehow Mrs Dunn made Andi feel like she was failing the cause of all sensible women in the country. Still the anticipation of this "fiery spectacular" as Mrs Dunn had put it, was too great. They had waited a long time to watch this junk go up in flames.

To Andi this event was very symbolic. It was burning away the useless stuff of their past and moving on with the good, the clean, the restored. *It's a lot like how God works in my life,* she thought philosophically as they stood under the awning of Harry's shed. *Jesus gets rid of the junk and keeps what is good.* Mr Dunn fanned the coals into life and soon the pile was smoking and flames were licking up over old mattresses and broken shutters and rotten timber. *When Jesus gets rid of the rubbish, it's a bit like he burns it – so we can never retrieve it. It's gone forever!* It is no mistake that the symbol of the Holy Spirit is a flame, thought Andi.

What occurred next, happened so fast. As Mr Dunn bent down to flick a burning piece of lattice into the fire, he gave out a bellow that made every one flinch. When he stood up there was a death adder clinging to the back of his hand. His face had gone deathly pale as he grabbed it by the body and yanked it free. He flung it wide into the heat of the fire and staggered into Harry's arms.

* * *

11

Harry swept up his father like a small child and ran to the house kicking in the door. "Ma! Ma!" he yelled as he put him down on Jo's bed. "Tell her what's going on," he pleaded to the girls as he bounded out the door to fetch Dr Larsen. He leapt onto his saddled horse and tore off down the road, dust kicking up urgently.

Mrs Dunn stood frozen in the doorway for a moment. She saw the tears of the girls and the ashen face of Daisy and the bloodied puncture marks on the back of her husband's hand. Mr Dunn licked his lips, dry from the heat of the fire. "Now Margaret," he said in a husky voice, "it ain't no body's fault. It's happened to better men than me. We all have our time to answer the call…"

Margaret suddenly thawed. "Well, this isn't your time Harold Dunn! So, don't you go confessin' that it is! Knife! Water! Hot water! Now!" She barked out commands like an army commander and Daisy whirled into motion. In seconds she was back with the butcher's knife that Mrs Dunn had lent them to prepare their meal, and a small bowl of water in an enamel basin. Margaret grabbed her husband's hand and slit it across the snakebite. It bled freely. She pumped at the arm trying to get it to bleed more.

There was blood everywhere. Andi struggled out of the room and collapsed on the lounge; her face ashen.

Jo ran and got some spare sheets and their one and only spare towel. "How is this going to help?" asked Jo looking in dismay at all the blood.

Daisy quietly pursed her lips. "Maybe she can get rid of the poison. Maybe… before it gets into his body," she said as she passed another sheet.

Dr Arthur Larsen walked quickly up the front stairs. This job was sometimes more than he could bear. How could he tell his closest neighbour that there is nothing he could do? *More* people die from a death-adder bite than live. Everybody knows that, but how do you tell them that he has *never* seen anyone survive a deep bite – like Harry had described this one.

He sat beside the bed and bandaged up the knife wound firmly and helped clean up the mess. He didn't want his patient looking like a murder victim when Sister Bernie got here. Then he got out his bag and went to give him an injection. Mr Dunn shook his head. "Now Arthur, I'm not goin' to die drugged. I just want to be with my fine family. I have precious few minutes… promise me you won't give me the opiate. It don't hurt so bad… just a dull aching there. Margaret's done more damage than the adder, me thinks," he said with an ironical twist of a smile.

The doctor sighed and put away the medicines in his bag. He would honour his friend's wish. He believed dying men should have whatever they want, even pain.

Harry had gone straight from Dr Larsen' house to get Sister Bernie. The old missionary nurse would take care of everything. She had a wealth of knowledge and experience. Arthur went out to the kitchen and put the kettle on the stove and stoked the fire. A cup of tea… that's what they needed. It is the best medicine for waiting. Then he sat down on a kitchen chair and prayed. Dr Larsen knew God took over where medicine gave out. "Lord God in Heaven, this man is one of your finest servants. God help us! If there is something, anything that can be done, God in Heaven please save him, because I'm not wanting to bury this man. Not this one. No!"

Harry came back breathless, and shortly after Sister Bernie rode up calmly on a horse. She was a thin, strong woman with white hair and a weathered face full of wrinkles. She had bright eyes and a firm mouth that told you she would not tolerate nonsense, and at the same time – just possibly, that she was capable of a great deal of mischief.

Dr Larsen met her at the gate and helped her dismount. "Sister thank you for coming so soon. It's a bad bite. I want you to look after him. Make sure he gets everything he needs."

She looked at his face. The years of caring had made his eyes crease in worry lines. "When was he bitten?"

"About thirty minutes ago. The paralysis has not started yet."

"Is Margaret here?"

He nodded in response.

"Doctor," Sister Bernie paused; and then shrugged as if there was nothing to lose. He looked at her eyes. They were thoughtful, kind eyes – not hardened, even by a lifetime of nursing the sick and witnessing so much pain. Her mind was thinking, thinking hard… "Doctor – it is the paralysis that finally kills them with a death adder, is it not? Not like the brown snake – where they bleed…"

"Yes," he said. "Not everyone has reached agreement with that… but I have seen enough to believe it to be so."

"Mr Dunn is healthy, fit… even for his age. He is tough. If we can nurse him through the paralysis, and his heart does not give out… he may survive. I know he could."

"It was a bad bite. Margaret bled it some."

"Not too much I hope. He needs his blood. Don't want him going into shock as well."

"She cut it – but it was on the back of his hand… it

didn't bleed greatly."

"Doctor... I have heard of a contraption... one they are developing to use in infantile paralysis. It breathes for the patient when they cannot breathe for themselves. I think it could support him."

Doctor Larsen looked at her. "I have read about the Drinker machine... the one developed by the American researcher. He wants to use it in polio treatment."

"Yes," she said excitedly, "they are calling it the 'iron lung'... because it breathes for the patient whose diaphragm and other muscles are weak. It looks like an iron drum with a bed inside where the patient lies. The pressure sucks out the chest wall, and the patient breathes in air."

"But there is no such machine in Australia... certainly none in Gum Ridge. I doubt they are even available in clinics in America yet." The reality of their isolation in rural Australia was a harsh one.

But to Sister Bernie bush-ingenuity was a greater reality. "I was thinking about Harry's workshop... if we told him what the lung was, he could make one! It will be rudimentary at best... and we have only five or six hours until the paralysis sets in... but it may be enough to get him through the next 36 hours, even if we have to manually pump the bellows."

Suddenly Dr Larsen felt very tired. "Sister, this man

is not just my patient – he is my friend… and I am all out of ideas. One day I hope there will be a miracle medicine… one that will neutralize snake toxin, or absorb it, or something… but that day is not today." He paused and sighed heavily. "I will try even something as bizarre as this 'iron-lung' idea of yours, if it offers just a flicker of hope. It is worth a try. I'm sure Harry would try to fly to the moon backwards if it has even a remote chance of helping his father." The doctor turned to go inside. Sister Bernie held his arm lightly, retaining him. "Yes Sister?"

"It may not work. Harry must understand that if it fails, or if we can't get it to operate well enough, it is not his fault. That is a big thing for a son to carry for the rest of his life."

"We can but try. Sister – you are a praying woman… use your influence."

She brushed passed him then. "And what makes you think for one second I haven't been pleading with the Almighty for this man's life since Harry came to me?"

* * *

Harry stood by the bed with the sketches that Sr Bernie and Dr Larsen had made. "Pa, I'm going out to the shed a while… to build a breathing machine. Sister reckons it may help later. So, you lie calm and we'll be back as soon as we can." He nodded to Jo. "Do ya reckon Andi will be okay? I could do with some help."

As he left the room, Harold senior smiled at Larsen. "You're a wise man Doc. Not just smart – but wise. It's just what the boy needs. A project to keep him occupied."

Arthur stood up then. "Harold, I don't usually contradict my patients, but I *will* contradict my friend. This is not just a "project" to distract his worry. It may be the difference between you seeing tomorrow or seeing Glory. We have to give it a try. The poison *is* in your system. I can't get rid of the toxin, so we have to treat what it does. Is it going up your arm yet?"

"No Doc. Not that I can feel. Mind you – the way Margaret slashed it about, I'm not sure I would know."

He just shrugged. "I think you will know."

Sister Bernie stood in the corner giving Margaret a hug. The little nurse was almost swallowed by her enormous embrace. Sister Bernie sat Mrs Dunn down by her husband's bed and told her to hold Harold's good hand. "Now Margaret, just be telling your man to stay calm and strong. He'll get to the point where he won't be able to talk sense, but his hearing will stay clear. You keep sayin' you love him. They are mighty powerful words."

She turned her attention to Daisy who tried to disappear into the shadows. As far as Daisy was concerned this whole day was a nightmare. Everyone in this superstitious town will believe this incident was the condemnation of God, paying out judgement on this family for coming to eat at her house. She said the dinner and the bon-fire was a stupid idea from the start. This is what she gets for giving in a little bit. She should have stayed strong and put her foot down.

Sister Bernie looked at her grimly. Daisy stared back. That's all she needed: an old, religious, retired, missionary nurse getting on her case as well. Why couldn't they all just leave her alone!

"Miss Brown, Margaret needs to stay with her husband, so I will ask you to help with the work that needs to be done. First, we need a board – an old door or something, that we can put under this mattress. The springs sag badly."

Daisy stared at her. That was hardly her fault. Was she to be blamed for everything – even an inadequate bed? Next, they'll say she planted the snake and planned the whole thing. They'd love to make it into a crime and lock her away.

"Miss Brown, I know this is hard, but we have to work together. Do you have an old door that we can use on the bed?"

Daisy opened her eyes wide, her long lashes looking dramatic in the dim light. She could be playing a part in a horror stage play. This was so surreal. Mr Dunn did not deserve this. Perhaps the town people were right – perhaps *she* should be lying on the bed preparing to die instead.

Sister Bernie came over and gave her a gentle shake by the shoulders. "Daisy! A bed board! Tell me what you have. We can use any door… even one that is still swinging - if needs be."

Slowly Daisy focused… and miraculously remembered the old toilet door that had fallen off the out-house. They had debated about tossing it on the bon-fire but they decided to use it to make a table near the laundry copper. She took Sister Bernie outside to help carry it in.

* * *

Harry stood momentarily by the blacksmithing forge with the drawings in his hand. He was not sure that he could do this. He could pull down an engine and rebuild it, but how do you make something that isn't even invented yet? He looked at the sketches but all he saw was his father's kind eyes telling him that he was the proudest father on earth and the luckiest man alive. A strange thing for a man to say, when his life was about to slide dramatically away, thought Harry. But that was so like Pa. Some people command regard. His Pa was one of those men. He tried to swallow an enormous lump in his throat, but it hovered at the back of his tongue, the emotion choking him.

Andi came over and touched his sleeve. "Harry?" she prompted, but he didn't respond and just turned away. Jo signalled for Andi to take the diagrams out of his hand. Jo grabbed an enamel mug hanging on a nail and dipped it in the small barrel of water by the forge used to cool red hot metal. She tossed it full in his face. Harry jumped and blinked the water out of his brown eyes.

"What did ya do that for?"

"Harry – we have to start! There is hardly any time… every minute is important. That's what Dr Larsen said."

"Fine thing for you to say! This is impossible."

Andi stepped forward. "God's good at impossible. There must be a way…" she coaxed.

Suddenly Harry felt the pressure was going to explode in his head. "If there is a way – it is not impossible! Don't you get it? It can't be done!"

"Well actually," said Andi quite logically, "It can be done. *I've* even heard of these iron lung machine things."

He stared at her wide eyed. Was he really so disconnected with the world that a kid knew more about what exists out there, than he did? "Well, *I* haven't, and I certainly haven't *built* one."

"Whimp!" said Jo disgustedly. "We'll do it without you then," She wasn't going to stand around when something could help Mr Dunn. She needed to *do* something; and this something may help.

Andi held the plan in her hand. "We need a drum… big enough to fit a person inside… a big oil drum size would work wouldn't it?"

"That would be too short to fit a man inside… even if I had one." At Harry's garage, fuel was only supplied in 4-gallon square tins that were delivered in wooden boxes. Big drums and bowser fuel hadn't come to the regional areas yet. They could manufacture a drum that size out of flattened smaller tins – but they didn't have enough time for that now. Quite insidiously Harry was drawn into problem solving.

Andi stood up. "The rat barrel! That would do it. I don't suppose it *has* to be iron to be an "iron lung". If we cut it in half long ways… it can go over him on the bed."

"Too short," said Jo.

"But does that matter? You only breath with your chest… it doesn't have to cover your legs. If it goes around his neck – it'll reach past his waist.

"If we cut it – how do you seal it? It's got to be tight to make the vacuum." Slowly they worked through the problems. Harry had already gone and got the barrel and was cutting it down the middle. Once they started, the ideas flowed. They used a heavy canvas wagon cover to make tight curtains for the ends to fit around his neck and waist.

They cut up more canvas and wrapped it around a thin rod and nailed it down the side to slide underneath Mr Dunn's back to encase him in it completely.

"We can't seal it all around yet. We have to get him in it…" reminded Andi.

Then Harry disconnected his bellows he had not long installed on his blacksmithing forge and fitted them to a hole in the side of the barrel.

Won't it end up pumping so much air into the barrel that it will blow up like a balloon?" said Jo. Her lack of scientific processing skills made this seem quite a logical outcome.

"We seal it, and block the valve at the back, we'll only be using the air that is inside the barrel. It will be normal pressure… until we open the bellows and it sucks the air out – creating the negative pressure the Doc wants for his chest to expand… he reckons that will make him breath. We pump the bellows and the same amount of air goes back into the barrel. Closed system. God, I hope this works!" And both Jo and Andi knew Harry wasn't swearing: it was a prayer.

They turned and saw Daisy standing at the door of the shed as the setting sunlight streamed in through the door behind her. She looked uncomfortable, like a child caught in the pantry. She had never been to the shed before.

She said, "Sister Bernie wants to know how you're going. It's nearly been five hours… his speech is slurring and he's … he's… weak."

* * *

Slowly the machine was reassembled in the bedroom in the light of a kerosene lamp by the bed. Sister Bernie stood quietly by the foot of the bed, her lips moving silently. She checked his pulse and rolled over his hand. A violent red streak was visible up his arm and spread onto his chest. "Harry'sss… look'ssss after your'ssss Ma."

Sister Bernie moved close to the bed. "Harold… don't be talking… Everything you've ever said will be enough for now."

He closed his eyes. Time ticked slowly on. His face became like a mask… lifeless almost. He tried to say something…but only an incoherent slur of sounds came from his throat. Margaret patted his other hand and held it tightly. "I love you Harold Dunn - don't you dare go leaving me yet!" Jo thought that if Harry had any choice in the matter, he wouldn't be game to defy her. She sounded really ticked off.

Everyone stood in the lounge room except Mrs Dunn. They were whispering – like they were talking around a dead person. Dr Larsen nodded. "We'll have to try the machine. His respirations are barely…" He had hoped against hope he was wrong and it wasn't a severe bite. He had hoped the patient would start to pull out of it before they needed to intervene. He handed over to Sister Bernie. "How do you want to work it Sister?"

Sister Bernie was definite. "Harry will work the bellows for twenty minutes, the rest of us will do ten... and then rotate back around. Slow... remember a man only breathes 16 to 20 times a minute."

Harry closed his eyes for a second. He had attached the bellows and checked the seals around the drum. He lifted the bellows apart, the air sucking out of the barrel into the bag, and then slowly he squeezed the handles together again. Sister Bernie sat near the head of the bed and slid her arm down inside the canvas curtain around his neck. She rested her cheek above his mouth to feel any movement of air.

Swiiiish, hooooo, swiiiish. The air whooshed into the bellows creating a vacuum in the barrel... hooooo... the air flowed back. Harry searched Sister Bernie's face as she concentrated hard. Slowly she nodded. "Yes, it's making a difference... just keep it nice and slow..." Swiiiish, hooooo, swiiiish, hooooo. Up and down - slowly, rhythmically, Harry began to breathe for his father.

* * *

12

Mr Dunn stirred in his bed as the early dawn peeked in through the window. "Smoke… I smell smoke…" he whispered hoarsely.

Sister Bernie shook herself awake and was at his side immediately. After two and a half days of sleepless supervision she had finally succumbed to closing her eyes in a straight back chair beside the windowsill. "Smoke?" she said. The air pumped through the forge bellows smelt of smoke. She checked his pulse – it was now stronger and rhythmic… still a little slow perhaps, but quite acceptable. His breathing had been getting stronger and stronger each hour. Finally, they pulled away the machine.

Mr Dunn stretched his arms and tried to swing his legs out over the side of the bed, but they wobbled unsteadily. Sister Bernie settled him back on a collection of thin, lumpy pillows. "I take it you are feeling better Harold?" she questioned.

His voice still slurred, but they could make out words. "My hand feels like it's been ripped off. Everything feels wrong, but other than that… I smell smoke… I'm sure…" He looked puzzled. "Smoke…" he repeated, half to himself.

Margaret sat upright, the dark circles under her eyes telling of the faithful vigil she had made. "Harold – the girls got you to set a fire… that's what caused this debacle to start with!"

"Now Margaret," he interrupted quietly, barely above a whisper, "it ain't nobody's fault. All's well, that ends well."

Harry was on the lounge sleeping out of exhaustion and relief. Jo had squeezed in beside Andi… and both were so tired they hadn't moved an inch. Everyone was abruptly awoken when a deafening explosion suddenly split the air. The glass in the window shattered onto the chair where Sister Bernie had been dozing just minutes before. Everyone was running, even before they had a chance to wake up. Some of the town's people came panting up the street still in their night-shirts, past the house, pointing to Harry's shed.

Smoke billowed out of the large door in dark, ugly clumps. Harry was dancing around on the verandah in his long-johns trying to pull boots on his bare feet. He jumped the fence and bounded towards the shed door, yelling for someone to get the fire cart. Already someone was hitching up a team to pull the tank, but it was not needed. A half dozen men already had it pulled through the street. Someone else was in the school yard ringing the bell continuously.

Harry stood there momentarily deciding whether to cut his losses and let it burn. "Can't beat this one out with a bag. The fire cart won't be long. Only have a small amount of fuel in there thank goodness..." he said to no one in particular as Jo and Andi ran up beside him.

Suddenly he stood stock still. "What the....?" he muttered. Abruptly Harry covered his mouth with a handkerchief and dove into the inky depths of the smoke congested shed. He emerged with little Ruby limp in his arms. Soot smeared their faces and clothes, and her blond head stirred as they came into the fresh air.

She was whimpering something over and over. "What's she saying?" asked Andi, "Lady... pretty Baby? I don't know..."

"Maybe she means her doll. It might still be in there," offered Jo.

"Oh Ruby... we won't be able to get it..." said Andi apologetically.

Harry looked at the crumpled girl's little face. "Oh no..." he muttered to himself as he quickly glared at the shed, "she couldn't..." He gasped as the smoke billowed thicker from the doorway.

"Harry – you can't go back in there now. It's getting worse."

He ignored them. "Just take Ruby to Sister Bernie and then get her mother." He swallowed hard on the words as if they choked him, while tying his handkerchief around his face. Then he dived onto the ground and crawled back into the sooty clouds.

Jo and Andi gathered Ruby in their arms. They ran to Sister Bernie… too stunned to say anything. What was Ruby doing in Harry's shed? As they bounced up the stairs she started to sob. By the time they laid her on the lounge, Ruby was crying, lustily from shock and fear. Poor little mite. Jo sat down and Ruby clung to her like a limpet as Sister Bernie checked her over. She seemed fine but for a small graze on her arm. Andi ran past the gathering onlookers, down to the Post Office to fetch her parents.

Andi's chest felt like it would explode as her legs churned down the road. She burst through the shop door and the little bell tinkled uselessly. The store was deserted. "Hello?" called Andi anxiously banging on the counter. "Hello!" Had they gone up to the fire with everyone else? Is that how Ruby got to be inside the shed? It didn't seem to match the time needed.

Tentatively she walked behind the counter, calling out as she went. "Hello? I'm Andi from the Muldoon cottage – is anyone there?" Silence answered her as she went past the table and a huddle of small pieces of furniture crammed into the space that served as their living area. She looked curiously at Ruby's little red-haired doll squeezed into a cradle made from an old wooden apple crate covered with a patchwork rag quilt. She picked it up. "Hello?" she called again as she went out the back through the squeaky screen door. Piles of wooden boxes were stacked by the step. A scrap of newspaper and a few leaves blew around in a little willy-willy across the hard ground. She heard anxious voices coming towards her.

"Sid! She's never gone off like this… something terrible has happened. It's Daisy! I know it!"

"Gladys, calm down – I'll call the constable. We'll make a search…"

"Hello?" said Andi carefully, stepping out into the courtyard trying not to startle them as they came around the corner. "Hello? I've come to…"

She stared at the doll in her hands. "You! Where's Ruby?" Gladys pounced at Andi, grabbing at the doll, panic all over her face. "What have you done to her? We haven't got money if that is what you want!" Her husband held her back.

Andi retreated; her eyes wide in disbelief. "I came to tell you we found her! What did you think? That we'd kidnapped her? You've got to be kidding!"

Sidney stared through his eyeglasses. "You *found*

Ruby? Where?"

Gladys leapt forward and shook her. "Is she okay? She's *never* gone away like this before! She wouldn't do that!"

Andy jumped back. "She's fine, just fine… a little shaken, but…"

"Oh Sidney! Oh, I've got to see her… my baby!"

Andi quickly reassured them. "She's fine. Sister Bernie has checked her and there's nothing… a little scratch on her arm, that's all."

"I've got to go to her!"

"She's with the others at the Muldoon cottage."

"With Daisy? Oh Sidney – no!"

Andi looked at this overwrought pair and tried to measure her words. "I wouldn't worry too much. Daisy wasn't even out of bed when we left… even with all the fuss about the fire she didn't emerge…"

"Fire! Oh, my baby! What have you done?"

"Ruby's with Sister Bernie and Mrs Dunn… and Jo. She's perfectly safe."

* * *

The onlookers stared at the shed in horror. Another explosion rocked the ground and the doorway spewed out more black smoke and bits of flying debris, pushing back those who stood ready to go inside to pull Harry out. Mrs

Dunn went pale as the gathering crowd under the window of Mr Dunn's sick room murmured about Harry's heroic rescue mission for Ruby's doll. "Harold – I don't know where that son of yours gets his scatterbrain ideas. I'd make the girl a doll myself if that is all it was. We can replace dolls."

Harold shook his head knowingly. "You know he's the girl's god-father. He's got a special place in his heart for that little angel. He'd do anything for Ruby."

"Even kill himself? It's ridiculous. It's just a toy. He should count his blessings that the girl is safe." Her mother's eyes scanned the black clouds anxiously, searching for movement. The billowing mass seemed to confirm the certainty the explosion had blasted him.

"Half the world sacrificed themselves in a war they didn't invent or even understand. What makes you think Harry would do less for someone he loves?" said Mr Dunn quietly.

"Can't someone go in after him?"

"I'd go myself, except my legs don't work properly."

Sister Bernie came over and stood beside them. "The girl's parents are here," she said as they burst into the room.

"Ruby! Darling!" Little Ruby ran to her mother's arms amidst cries and tears of relief. Gladys gently handed Ruby her little red-haired doll. Margaret looked in bewilderment as the little girl hugged and kissed and squeezed her doll with delight.

Gladys grimly acknowledged Margaret's stares. "I knew something was wrong. She never goes anywhere without Ruby-Rae. This doll is her very best friend."

"But if she has the doll… then Harry is looking for something that's not in there!"

Cheers erupted outside. Andi and Jo tried to see past the huddle of people at the fence. Men were poised with a canvas stretcher. One group dived in past the cloud to drag Harry away from the heat and smoke. Another group of men started pouring water on the shed from the water cart as its driver rushed up. Harry had crawled out like a Saint Bernard rescue dog, and with him was Daisy. Her wrists were bound together with rag, her arms draped over his neck like a halter, her limp body dragging on her coat that slid underneath him like a sled. When they lifted her up, a doll with a celluloid face, dressed in feathers and frills, rolled out from the pocket of her coat.

* * *

Harry lay on Andi's bed next to his father still resting on Jo's bed. Soot covered his body and he coughed spasmodically. Burns covered his arms and hands, and there was a violent looking gash on his forehead. Sister Bernie put him in a cool bath and told Margaret how to tend the burns on his arms, meticulously picking the dirt from the wounds with a pair of tweezers. When she was done, his mother sat by his bed shaking her head in disbelief. "In just a few days I nearly was left a childless widow! First my husband and then my son. Praise be to God, He had mercy on me – on both accounts."

Sister Bernie tended Daisy in her own room. She had regained consciousness but still muttered deliriously every so often. Restlessly she would call out and become agitated. Dr Larsen gave her medication. She was in a lot of pain from burns to her neck and limbs. Her arm was broken and badly displaced from being dragged from the shed. Rather than submit her to the arduous trip into a hospital, Dr Larsen set the bones in place there.

After a few days Harry came in to visit Daisy before they left to go back home. His father only complained that the snake-bite site was intensely itchy. He carried a grey, unwell look about him, but there was a wry sort of humour that sat on his lips. "The thing is," Mr Dunn had said, "I've been poisoned by one of the known world's deadliest toxins. Guess it's going to take a while to seem like me old self again…"

Harry's arms were bandaged to the tops of his shoulders, in clean sheeting and the gash on his forehead was puckering tight where the drying sutures pulled at the skin.

Daisy looked through swollen puffy eyes at Harry. "You had no right," she accused angrily.

"No right to do what?" he asked quietly, even though he suspected what she meant.

She stared sullenly passed him to Sister Bernie where she had retreated to the corner of the room. "I'm here Daisy – I won't leave," she said quietly.

Daisy said nothing for a long time. Harry was never intimidated by silence. He waited for her to continue. After a while Daisy squirmed and grunted uncomfortably. "You know jolly well what! It would have saved everyone a whole lot of trouble if you'd left me there!"

"Daisy – I wasn't about to stand by and consult the will of the town. You needed help. How can you think there was even a choice?"

"You smug, self-righteous…" her anger bubbled over and she was unable to say anything further. Most of her burns were slight, but the bad ones were in various stages of crusting and weeping. The pain from stretching the skin by her jerky movements silenced her.

"I'm sorry you are hurt. But I'd do it again …" said Harry firmly.

"Why?" she screamed again. "You don't get it! Are you dense or just a stubborn old mule? Can't you see it would be better for everyone – especially Ruby!"

The mention of Ruby was like a slap on the face. He winced and stood still. "Well then," he said slowly, "I must be dense – because for the life of me I cannot see how that little girl is better off without you in her life."

Tears welled in her eyes. "I'm tired Harry. Go away."

Sister Bernie showed him to the front door. "Son – there is a fine line between grace and pity. You have such a great capacity for grace. Don't cloud that gift with pity – so that it makes you think you love this girl. She is not ready. And as it is, I suspect it will break your heart and steal away your grace."

Harry stared at this little white-haired woman with a stunned expression. He blinked hard and tried to comprehend what she was saying. Love Daisy? Out of pity? He walked briskly to the buggy that his father had ready to take them home. There was no way he would love Daisy out of pity. She was not his type… she was a city girl now. But more importantly than that – her heart did not belong to God. They could *never* see heart to heart on anything. He had no intention of loving any girl who did not love God first. She was not even an option.

* * *

13

The next day Harry quietly inspected the damage to the shed. It had been saved... quite unaccountably. Everyone said it should have burnt to the ground, but the frame stood strong and intact. Much of the iron was salvageable as well as many of the tools and benches inside. Constable Langford came and vied him for information.

"There is a question of arson, Harry. We will need to investigate," he said writing some notations in his book.

"I was helping Sister Bernie and the Doctor with Dad. They both can account for my being there," he said deliberately inspecting the bandaged burns on his arms.

"Wasn't necessarily suggesting that you..."

"No one was hurt," he said cutting him off, "I will not be pressing charges."

"But your insurance? This will definitely affect your..."

"Bob – it wasn't insured. It's not an issue."

The constable stopped and looked at him. "No insurance?"

"A question of economics Bob. Who can afford it? It was a risk, but one I took with my eyes wide open."

"But Daisy Brown had to have set that fire. It's a

criminal act."

"Are you going to charge her – without me pressing for it?"

Bob Langford looked at him. "Harry Dunn you are a piece of work. No one else in this shire would consider letting her off. I don't know that I can…"

Harry said nothing, but he acknowledged the truth of what the constable said. Perhaps he did pity her after all.

The constable continued. "Then there is that mess with Sid and Glad's little girl. They want her locked up. I really don't see how we can't."

"Bob – you gotta do your job, and I don't presume to understand the ins and outs of the law. I just want you to see if could push for some leniency with the judge. I have to rebuild the shed… that's a given… and the garage will benefit the community. Perhaps if she had to do some supervised service; help rebuild it, the courts might see it as justice done?" It was a long shot, but Harry didn't see how locking her up would help reform or heal her wounds. Daisy was just too sad, and she needed much more than a view of iron bars to bring about change.

* * *

Jo and Andi helped Sister Bernie look after Daisy. She wouldn't relax her decree that they were not to step inside her room, but the old nurse was given privileges.

They would sit outside as Sister Bernie dressed Daisy's burns and listen to her whimper as Sister Bernie took off the bandages and reapplied fresh ones. It was their job to boil the soiled linen dressings up in the copper. One afternoon Andi sat on the verandah on a couple of old cane chairs with Jo rolling clean bandages. "You know, it doesn't make sense," Andi said quite puzzled. "Sister Bernie comes in here – takes over Daisy's life and she doesn't even object. With everyone else – she is completely shut off."

"Yeah – and it's not like Sister Bernie treads gently. For a little old lady – she stomps all over the place."

Andi chuckled. "I thought missionaries were supposed to be gentle, sweet, '*let's wipe your nose*' type of people."

"It's hard to imagine Sister Bernie wiping anyone's nose!"

Just then Sister Bernie appeared at the door with some afternoon tea on a tray. "May I join you ladies? I confess I was listening a bit," she said with a wink. Andi was mortified she had heard them talking. Sister Bernie just waved her wrinkled hand. "Ahh, you are actually right. I was never good at wiping snotty noses."

Andi blushed and Jo looked very impressed that someone her age could be so frank. Not that they knew what her age actually was. "But aren't you supposed to?

Since you were a missionary?" asked Jo with a grin. Andi looked the other way.

"I haven't read those rules anywhere. I think *missionary* is such a bogus term. It's really just location. My home was in India... simple as that. No one gets a personality change, just because they move house. Mind you, I do remember wiping a leper's nose once... but that was because he had no fingers... and only until we figured out a way for him to do it himself. Only did it once." She laughed, as if it was most insightful of the girls to work that out about her. She passed around some of Andi's ANZAC biscuits – Margaret's recipe. They were crunchy – not soft how Mrs Dunn made them. Still, after their ordeal, of sleeplessness, the sugar made them worthwhile.

Sister Bernie smiled kindly. "Daisy has asked me to tell you about the fire."

"Why doesn't she tell us herself," said Andi.

"Oh, she will. She asked if I would do it, but I told her this is her story to tell. Perhaps she is reluctant because she is ashamed, or afraid."

Jo laughed. "Daisy – afraid. Yeah right."

"Fear shows itself in lots of ways. Perhaps for Daisy it is in her independence."

Andi took another bite of an ANZAC and crunched the crumbs loudly. Sister Bernie dunked her biscuit and took a sip of tea. "Daisy is the brunt of a lot of gossip going around town. She wants you to hear her version first. Constable Langford will most likely come over tomorrow. You just tell him what you saw. Other than that, you have no need to be involved."

"How can you say that? We live here. We *are* involved."

Sister Bernie took another slow sip of tea. "I'm not sure how much you know. Daisy thinks it's not much because you have stayed."

"Well gee – there's a vote of confidence," said Jo.

Sister Bernie searched the depths of her cup. "Daisy may be convicted if Harry presses charges. Even if he doesn't, she still might be… That's why Daisy wants you to know."

"Know what?"

Daisy appeared at the door. "That I… I am grateful for your friendship."

Jo rolled her eyes. "So, *this* is what you call being friends? Never would have known otherwise."

Andi agreed. "Friends talk to each other. They listen…" Daisy had fallen hard from the pedestal that Andi had constructed at the movie festival. It was a lifetime ago. She didn't even want to remember it was the same person. Funny how, when you get to know some people, they are not at all what you think. And not in a good way.

Sister Bernie smiled. "Could you be friends to Daisy now, and listen to what she has to say?"

Jo shrugged, and Andi nodded.

Daisy came and sat on the step.

"Having people around is hard for me because I have no one. My father died when I was little. My mother was sick and my grandparents never recovered from my dad's death. They resented having to look after two young children. My brother was killed in the war. Everything I have known was ripped out from underneath me."

"You grew up here and you chose to leave…" said Jo. "You could have stayed where you had people to support you."

Andi interjected. "Jo – you know she hated it here. She had to leave if she was going to get into acting. That was twelve years ago. No wonder she hasn't been back. This place is a creative morgue!"

Sister Bernie raised her crinkled eyebrows. "Daisy had ambitions and the gumption to pursue them. I believe there is merit in that. Being ambitious is fine as long as it is for the right things. Besides, there are honourable ways to pursue goals, and then, there are ways that compromise God's best." She paused before nodding for Daisy to go on.

Daisy starting fiddling with her ring again in a nervous sort of habit. "In actual fact, I did come back to Gum Ridge... once – for a very short time... just overnight... about five years ago."

"Why?"

"Ruby."

"Ruby?" the girls said together.

"Ruby was born in a convent-hostel for unwed mothers. I brought her here after she was born and gave her to Gladys and Sid to look after. Gladys had been a good friend when we were in school. At the time I said it was just for a short time, but I never came back... until now."

Jo and Andi stared at each other in shock. Sister Bernie quietly continued. "I know the circumstances because Sid asked me to help with the baby. She was tiny and malnourished. Ruby has never been told Daisy is her birth mother. Sid and Gladys have raised her as their own."

"Ruby – is your daughter? But why would you want to hurt her? This story just gets sicker!"

"No, no, I didn't try to hurt her! I just wanted to see Ruby and spend some time with her because Gladys refused to let me have any contact. I showed her the doll I had made, and we came down to the shed for a picnic. It was out of the sun and out of the way. It was just meant to be for a short time. The doll was so pretty Ruby didn't hesitate…"

"Doll?"

"Yes, the doll with the celluloid face that we found it in the house. I fixed it up."

"That's what happened to it…" said Jo remembering picking up the dilapidated doll when they first came into the house.

"Only the face was any good. I made a soft body out of some of those old curtains, and clothes. I used part of the costume wig I had to give her real hair… so now the doll has dark curls."

"The doll has Princess Shahnaz's hair?" said Andi in surprise.

"I worked on the project for Ruby every spare minute you were out. I made all her dresses with buttons and beads and feathers from some of the clothes I brought with me. I was so pleased with the way it turned out."

"It is so beautiful." Sister Bernie said it as if she had done something quite remarkable.

"But I intended to smuggle Ruby back before anyone missed her, after our picnic I was going to give her the doll." She paused and sighed. "Then I was going to burn the shed and stay inside… just like Dad. That was the plan."

Sister Bernie looked incredibly sad and they knew she believed every word.

Tears welled up in Andi's eyes. No one should ever be that desperate. Not really – not if people were there to help. But in the same breath she knew that Daisy had shut herself off from any help. She was an island of pain… isolated in a sea of loneliness.

"You're kidding! Drama queen to the end!" exclaimed Jo, "But you didn't take Ruby back! Gee – what a piece of work! How could you hurt a beautiful kid like Ruby?" Jo sat there, anger seeping through her emotions like hot water.

"No – that was not it at all! I realised it was a mistake to take her there. I was about to cut the picnic short and take Ruby back home when I saw a snake! It was so close to where Ruby was sitting on the rug! I jumped up to snatch her away and knocked the lamp over. The fuel ran – that's how the explosion happened. I threw my body and blanket over Ruby but I don't remember anything else."

Sister Bernie sighed. "No doubt Daisy saved her life by using the blanket. As far as we can tell Daisy was knocked unconscious and Ruby crawled out from under her when Harry heard her crying."

Andi sat on the step beside Daisy and swiped at her eyes with her sleeve. Her heart felt torn as she realised the enormity of Daisy's pain and what she had done. She was Ruby's mother; the fire was a dreadful string of events that went terribly wrong. Daisy had wanted out, but in the end, it turned out worse for her. "Won't you be charged with *reckless endangerment* or *kidnapping*, or something? This is really serious."

Sister Bernie was sober. "You are right. It is very serious. I will be praying for a miracle."

Jo shook her head. That was too far-fetched! "Oh, give me a break. You don't deserve a miracle! How could you be so... so..."

Sister Bernie thoughtfully sipped the last of her tea. "No one ever *deserves* a miracle. It is God who chooses to be merciful. When I was in India, I saw God intervene with many miracles... it made all the hard days exciting – to experience part of what God was doing. But it was *never* about being deserving... just about His grace."

Andi's raised her wet eyes. "You saw real miracles? True? What sort of things?"

"A blind man got his sight back – no medicine or operations – just God: one day he was blind, the next he could see. I saw a baby brought in by his mother to the hospital. He was so close to dead it was impossible to do anything for him. Yet he lived. The leper I was talking about before – with no hands, he was able to work from the colony and support his family. We saw men walk with false legs they made for each other; people were given hope and peace and love. They were all miracles."

Andi went quite still. "I wish I'd been there..." she said wistfully.

Sister Bernie smiled. "It was wonderful – a privilege. But you know, our God who worked on behalf of those Indians is still the same God here and now. We have been part of amazing miracles this week."

Jo looked sceptical. "Yeah – but we still had to use a machine..."

Sister Bernie gave no ground. "My child – do you know how remarkable that is? There is no accounting for the idea in the first place, or that Dr Larsen had just been reading about the Drinker machine, or Harry was able to build it, or even that the thing worked well enough to make a difference. Then we had enough people to pump it around the clock. It was indeed a miracle!"

"Well," said Jo, "When you put it like that..."

"And..." continued Sister Bernie, "Ruby, Daisy and Harry were saved from the fire. The fact the shed was not guttered is another evidence of God's kindness."

"But the burns..." objected Andi, looking at the bandages on Daisy's arms and the agonised cries that Daisy made every time Sister Bernie changed her dressings.

Sister Bernie looked at her softly, the lines around her eyes gathering in a million creases. "You know – I heard of a man's limbs growing back at another mission station. There was a young girl with us – a beautiful child – I prayed for such a miracle for her and I had so much faith that it would be so. I was sure her limbs would be restored... but God chose not to. I couldn't understand that. Did God love that other man more? Mr Dunn survived his death adder bite – does God love him more than old Mr Lacy or the little Chaney baby? Daisy survived a fire, but her father did not. I don't understand these things any more *now* than I did then. Perhaps part of it was because there was no one to pray – to push back the devil's plans to rob and destroy..."

"You think our prayers make that much difference?"

"I know they do child. Otherwise, why would Jesus spend so much time teaching us about prayer? But God is not a machine to crank start so we know exactly how He will work. He wants us to talk with Him. He wants to be part of our lives... the good bits and the sad bits."

Jo frowned. "It hardly seems fair... how some get a proper miracle and someone else doesn't."

Sister Bernie placed her teacup on the tray and looked directly at Daisy. "One thing I have come to trust is the Bible that says *'all things work together for good, to those who are called according to His purpose'*. God can turn everything around so something positive comes out of it. That's why

He is God."

"What happened to the doll – was it burnt in the shed?" ask Andi.

"No – I had it in my coat. It was saved.

"Well, after all that, at least Ruby gets to have her new doll," said Jo.

Sister Bernie shook her head. "No, I'm afraid not."

Daisy stood and swiped at her eyes. "Glad and Sid have refused to receive anything at all that is connected to me," she said sadly.

* * *

14

Andi didn't pretend to understand how any good could be worked out of the tragedy of Daisy's depression and circumstances. But she went on praying. She figured that if a spiritual heavy-weight like Sister Bernie didn't have all the answers and could still confidently say that prayer made a difference, that was at least a good place to start.

Daisy did go to court. She was taken to a larger town courthouse on the train with Constable Langford and Sister Bernie went along to dress her burns. Harry had long removed his dressings although he protected the pink, tender new skin carefully with long cotton shirts. But Daisy's broken arm and dislocated shoulder complicated the care of some of the less severe burns. She still kept on all her bandages and Sister Bernie continued to apply her special burn concoction made from a recipe that she had been given from an old Asian healer.

While they were away Harry started to clean up the shed. His arms were stiff from the burns, but Jo thought his stubborn neck was stiffer. He obstinately went about the ashes and twisted iron, sorting out what was salvageable and what was rubbish fill. Mr Dunn came down to help him cart things over to the wagon. Andi and Jo donned their oldest clothes and pitched in to give them a hand.

They had never seen Harry so agitated. He muttered loudly when he cut his hand on some sooty iron and wrapped it up roughly with his charcoal smeared handkerchief. When he was building the shed, they saw Harry silently watch his thumbnail go black when he accidentally bashed it with a hammer. But there was no silence today. He lost his footing stepping around some rubble and flew into an awful temper - kicking stuff left, right and centre.

"I reckon I might take this load to the dump and then I'll go and give your mother a hand with the tomatoes," said Mr Dunn staring at Harry as if he was looking at a total stranger. "I'm thinking he might be needing some time by himself to clear the air," Mr Dunn confided to the girls as he settled himself in the wagon. He tired easily and paced his workload to get through. He didn't have the energy for confrontation so with a flick of the reigns he steered the wagon towards their farmhouse.

Andi and Jo waved silently as he disappeared down the road. Andi looked at Jo with a shrug. "Does that mean we should leave too?" Harry was still noisily flinging things around.

"We could get something to eat," suggested Jo. "Harry – want a cup of tea?"

He looked sort of shocked, as if he had forgotten he was not alone. "Huh," he grunted, and briefly shrugged. He extracted a plank to sit on when the girls came back with some smoko. They settled in amongst the soot and sipped enamel mugs of billy tea. Everything was black today: the charred shed, the black plank they sat on, the black cup of tea, the burnt biscuits, and worse of all – Harry's mood.

"So, I guess you're regretting being lenient? This is kind of a mess," said Andi trying to bait him into talking.

"It's a *terrible* mess!" he asserted vehemently and scowled hotly into his mug.

Jo shrugged and then glared at him. "Harry! What is with you? You've had worse!" Jo began to launch into ways they could systematically attack the practical problem of the clean-up.

Andi stared at Harry's frustrated eyes, something dawning on her. She jabbed Jo firmly in the ribs and she pulled away glaring. "It's not the shed," Andi whispered.

"Then what?" Jo hissed back.

"Harry – we're going to get some more biscuits. Back in a tick." Andi dragged Jo back over to the house. "Jo it's not the fire that's driving him mad." When Jo stared at her blankly, Andi leant over and quietly whispered, "I think it's Daisy."

"Well, dah – you're the genius. Of course, it's Daisy.

She *burnt down* his shed!"

Andi shook her head. "Ah – uh."

"What do you mean? Of course, she…" said Jo mystified as Andi raised her eyebrows and shrugged her shoulders knowingly. Jo starred at her for a while. "Nooo! You don't think?" she gasped in disbelief.

Andi nodded. "Yep. I reckon he is."

Jo groaned. "That's terrible. He can't love *her*! Well, I know you're supposed to love everyone – but "*Love*"? He's so decent and she's sooo…. so…. well, so Daisy!"

"Not to mention she's in court as we speak... and then there is Ruby… and, oh boy. Harry is so right. This is a terrible mess!"

* * *

"Do you think Daisy came to Gum Ridge just to get custody of Ruby?" mused Jo as they sat on the front step looking dejectedly over towards the smoke stained shed. She hated being taken for a schmuck, but that's exactly how she felt. Daisy had summed them up and used them. So much for all the appreciation for being friends. Perhaps she thought they offered some sort of distraction aside from her infamous reputation – which was quite deservedly acquired, it seemed. "I bet this turns out to be one of those custody battles when no one wins and the kid gets all the losing," Jo concluded in despair.

"No!" said Andi with sudden fervency "No! It won't be like that at all! I will pray that something better will come even out of this mess... for Ruby, and Harry... and even for Daisy, and Sid and Gladys too. They are so hell bent on revenge! I still bet Sister Bernie reckons God can work things out for good even here... especially for Ruby."

"But Harry's the only one we know is a Christian. Did you ever think God might not want to... you know...?"

"You know... what?"

"Well, you know... mess with people's lives who don't much believe in Him."

"Jo, why would you think that? He loves everyone!" Andi looked totally scandalised.

"But these people might not like God... or want Him involved." *I don't know if I do believe... particularly...* she added quietly to herself. Sometimes Andi was so dense. She seemed to forget that Jo didn't share her uncompromising believe in her Good Father God. As far as Jo could tell, if God was like a father... then that's not an endorsement.

"Well we,... *I* am going to pray, that's all I know. God can work it out from there. After-all He *is* God. It's just like Sister Bernie said... you never know – He might want *us* to be part of it." Andi's eyes lit with her old energy that had been frequently absent since they had become entangled in Daisy and her depressing ways.

Jo grunted. "We *are* part of it and that's what I am afraid of," she said with a heavy dose of reluctance. "It's looking messier by the minute! Poor Ruby."

"Tell me you will pray with me Jo." Compassion filled Andi's eyes.

"Me? How can I pray? You know it's different for me Andi. After Sister Bernie talked with us, I thought it would be so simple... her being a Spiritual Heavyweight and all. But all I know now, is that I don't like things being messy - especially with kids involved. If it was just the adults stuffing things up – that would be easier. They're old enough to take it. Kids aren't."

"When the fall-out from the adult world involves children, isn't that all the more reason for us to be concerned?"

"Concerned? You think I'm not concerned?" Jo's eyes glowered. "Little Ruby is the sweetest little kid ever. Oh boy, it makes me mad! Madder than I get about anything!" Sparks fired dangerously hot in Jo's eyes.

Andi looked at her friend. "Jo - do you know what mum tells me? She says, 'Andi, don't waste it - don't waste all that energy *just* being angry!' she says, 'Turn your passion into positive prayers... and when you find the right direction: take positive action.'"

"But, how can I? I thought you said being angry was

sin. And since God is not in for sinners… I've kinda got no leg to stand on, because right now I am seriously pissed."

"The bible says, *'be angry and don't sin'*. Mum figures that means we can be angry about things because Jesus was. He was mad as a hornet's nest when they turned God's house into a Sunday market. And he was pretty ticked off when his disciples told those mothers to get lost and said he was too busy to see their children. Jesus loves kids. If we didn't get mad when they hurt, that would be messed up."

"Guess so…" Jo paused. Sometimes the intensity of her emotional flare-ups caused her to switch thoughts, automatically – as if to give herself some relief. "Do you know what else I hate? I hate those mushy paintings of Jesus sitting around with kids on a bowling-green lawn. They are always dressed in white like a studio photo – not a speck of dirt anywhere. Kids never sit still – and they never stay clean. None that I know of anyhow. I reckon they would have been running around in the dusty streets, having a wonderful game of tag and Jesus would have been 'it'!" Jo smiled at the picture that played in her mind. She wished she could have played tag with Jesus when she was a kid. The smile faded on her lips as she heard another voice. She restlessly got up and went back inside. She didn't want to think about that just now.

* * *

Andi and Jo decided to walk over to the Dunn farm and see how Harry was going. Margaret invited them in for supper. It was a sombre affair and Harry still hadn't come out of his room when they went to leave. "I'll drive you girls' home – it's just about dark," said Mr Dunn getting his hat.

"Could Harry drive us? We want to talk to him."

Harry reluctantly obliged. Such a direct request was hard to turn down. They sat on the bench seat and waited for him to adjust the harness. He jumped up and flicked the reigns silently. "What are you going to do Harry?" asked Andi directly.

"About what?"

"Daisy," she said.

"Not much," he muttered.

Jo reached over and poked him. "We know how you feel about her."

He glanced sideways at them and read their knowing expressions. He scoffed disdainfully. "Well I reckon there's nothing to know. Sister Bernie calls it pity."

"Is it?" asked Andi.

"Nope. I reckon not."

"So, what are you going to do?"

"Nothing. She ain't available..."

"What do you mean *not available*? Daisy's not

married... or is she?" asked Andi doubtfully. With Daisy anything was possible.

Harry looked at his friends as they drove down the road. Already the large clumps of cactus were crumbling like walls of the biblical city of Jericho. Harry had thought the prickly pear infestation would be the biggest crisis he would ever face. But now his heart told him otherwise. He shook his head. "Never married."

"Oh. You mean that she's had a baby." Silence. "Or that she's had to go to court?" More silence. "Because she burnt down the shed? Lied to you? She's sick and tried to suicide...." Jo would have kept going except Andi jabbed her hard with her elbow. "Still, all pretty sound reasons if you ask me," said Jo under her breath.

"What about forgiveness and second chances," said Andi, shocked that Harry would be so hard and uncompromising.

Harry stared straight ahead. "If that was all, it'd be as easy as pie. But it ain't. Her heart belongs elsewhere. That's the truth."

"Daisy loves someone else? Who? She never told us about anyone!" exclaimed Andi.

"Andi – you are forgetting that Daisy didn't speak to us at all... about anything," reminded Jo.

Harry sighed. He had always believed such things

were intentional, that one could choose where and how romance was initiated. But now he determined that even if the feelings were not planned, his behaviour would be deliberate. "I'm not courting a girl who doesn't love God. I can't believe the mess I'm in, and I don't even know how it happened, but it ain't right. I'll live with this for the rest of my life if I need to, but I'm choosing to do the right thing. And the proper thing is that my wife be a Christian woman first."

"Wow," said Jo quietly. "That's tough."

Harry nodded in the dark shadows of night. "It hurts like hell, but it would be far worse if I got hitched in the wrong way. I've thought it through long and hard. In the end it would be worse... far worse." Harry sighed and pulled the reigns to a halt in front of the Muldoon Cottage, and turned towards them in the dim evening light.

"Now you girls gotta swear on my grandmother's grave you'll never tell Daisy or anyone else for that matter. It is not for her to know, and if she ever finds out from me, I will have failed in my duty to God. Of course, she won't be back for a while yet... so it'll give me some thinking space."

Andi sat stock still gripping the edge of the cart. "Oh no! They're sending her to prison!" she gasped as the thought seeped into her consciousness.

"Prison? Na, they're not. Constable Langford came back today. Daisy has to stay to see some doctors. Sister Bernie has offered to supervise her, like on a parole sort of arrangement. She's got to do some community hours and also some hours to repair the shed. She won't go to prison. She has a restraining order – she can't see Ruby at all for six months... then it will be reviewed." Harry's voice sounded kind of flat... and he suddenly felt like he needed to go down to the beach and watch the moon-rise over the churning waves.

"Wow – I wonder if she realises that's a miracle," said Andi softly.

Harry flicked the reigns after the girls got out. "If she did, it would be a miracle indeed," he said as he turned to go home. Instead of taking the buggy through the farm gate, he unhitched the horse and flung himself on its bareback and reigned the horse around to go up to Murray's place. There was a ridge where he could look out to the east and watch the slither of moon rise in the east. It was a place where he could think. Now he regretted ever offering the shed reconstruction as a form of recompense. Suddenly it had turned into a punishment for him. How could he be with her and keep a lid on the emotions that whirled so close to the surface? She must never know, and if these two girls had figured it out so quickly, he was not sure he could do it.

But somehow, he must.

* * *

Harry sat on the rocky outcrop that jutted from the ridge staring through the stately arms of the gum trees that grew up below him. He watched the colours of dawn spread a ruby pink veil over the horizon. His mind had not stopped tossing and his heart was grieving. The sheer force of the emotions stunned him. Even if she was "available" she may never return his feelings. He could never marry Daisy without a miracle… he understood that. But now he also acknowledged that he probably would not marry anyone else. It would not be fair knowing his heart was romantically bound to another, however silently. His grief was for all the children he would never have; the shared vision and companionship that would never be his.

When Daisy left town twelve years ago, it was a relief. He thought then that time and space would free his heart to look elsewhere. But it was as if he had been made blind. He had thought time would take away the feelings… and it did in a way. Yet no other girl ever made an impression. He was single and unattached, and still he had always believed that one day he would be blessed with a wife and a family. This night he relinquished those ambitions. It was harder than anything he had ever had to do – even harder than deciding to go and work in the city.

He heard the train whistle blow in the clear morning air as it left the station and passed through the crossing. His heart pounded as he realised, he would listen for every train until he knew Daisy was home again… and safe.

* * *

Daisy stood in the shell of the workshop. Sister Bernie had covered her arm cast with old thick cotton stocking. She stared at the gaping holes in the walls and the roof and at the place where she had fallen. Andi and Jo stood quietly beside her. They had no idea what she was thinking. Her jaw was set firm and resolute. Harry had expected her to have some reaction about the arrangements: either to object or to thank him. She said nothing. The volatile Daisy he grew up with was nowhere to be found and it tore at Harry's heart. He passed her some gloves, conveniently ignoring the obvious hindrance that one hand was smothered in bandages holding a splint in place. "Sister Bernie thinks two hours a day will be enough to start with. You can choose to go straight through or do an hour each in the morning and afternoon." Harry was kind of relieved when she decided to just get it over and done with. Harry couldn't agree more.

Harry salvaged second-hand iron from old sheds and various chook houses around about. Neighbours pitched in and gave him whatever they could spare. Most admitted they weren't insured either and they knew everyone in the district would do the same for them. Slowly the shed was reconstructed. It lacked the new, stylish frontage now, but it had become embedded as a local icon anyway. Harry's shed was about visions and ambitions, perseverance, survival and pulling together.

There was one particular blessing Harry thanked God for: the bellows. They had still been in the house. Harry had not taken them back in the aftermath of exhaustion that hovered around his father's struggle for survival. He quickly set up his forge to be useable again so he could do as many blacksmithing jobs as came his way. This was far more his bread and butter than working on automobiles. He was keen to get everything in the shed completed so he could provide a mechanical service once again. He enjoyed this more than anything.

Daisy hardly spoke. Harry wished he could shake her, as if somehow that would pour life back into her listless eyes that had sunken dark circles under them. He tried to provoke her into showing some spirit. Even before her cast was removed, he continued to ask her to do things that he had quietly confirmed with Sister Bernie were not unreasonable. He was ruthless in extracting excellence in what he required of her, getting her to redo things until they were right. He never gave her any leeway or sympathy.

Sister Bernie was pleased the way strength was coming back into her arm. Daisy never objected. She just silently did what Harry required, sluggishly fulfilling whatever he wanted done.

Harry was amazed. Daisy would never have had such persistence or careful submission once. Occasionally he saw her eyes blaze, but she would never give in to whatever distressed her. He wondered if it was because she was so cowed by life, or if something important had changed within her. He didn't know, so he made a pact, with himself and God. *Whenever Daisy is here, I will pray. God, you can at least bless her where I cannot.*

So, pray he did… every nail and tool Daisy passed him, every sheet of iron she held, every piece of metal she heated on the forge or held in the tongs, was always shrouded in a mist of prayer and blessing. In the process, it returned a blessing on Harry. The progress on the shed seemed steady and sure. Before long he was hanging a newly painted sign that Daisy had printed: *'Harry's Shed. Open for Business."*

Larsen and the Telfords booked their motor-carriages in for maintenance, and Harry was advising newcomers in the field of automobile transport about the choice of vehicle. He even offered to act as agent for the purchasers and went on trips to the city to collect their cars and drive them home. With the setback from the fire he knew it would be a long time before he could afford to buy a vehicle of his own, so this was the next best thing.

Daisy had faithfully kept an account of her hours, and Harry signed them off at the end of each week. When it came time for Harry to release her from the work bond, he gave a sigh of gratitude. It was over.

But after three days Daisy came back. She stood silent and still in the shadow of the shed wall, waiting for him. She coughed, embarrassed. "Harry – I want to ask if I can come back to work. I'm used to being here and I want to be kept busy." She stumbled her way through the speech. She had never imagined that she'd miss being part of Harry's establishment. When she was counting her hours, it seemed like an interminable period of time the judge had allocated to Harry.

Harry turned away and sighed. He had thought he would be spared the constant demands that her presence made on him. It was not healthy. He couldn't do it forever.

Daisy heard the sigh. She felt sad, where once she would have been angry. Even Harry had tired of her. The force of community opinion had finally seeped through his iron-clad determination. "I can't let you be here…" Harry began slowly. He turned and faced her; his manner strained. He sighed again. He knew he would do whatever it took.

"You can't work, not anymore… without payment. The court agreement has been fulfilled. I'm not sure I make enough to employ someone, and it will mean I will have to charge rent if you take the job."

Daisy smiled with relief. "Great! We will work on that then." She didn't want to be stuck at home with nothing to occupy her mind and body. This was somehow important to her. She appreciated the way Harry was always straight and kind. It baffled her why Harry was different. He was caring when others were cruel. Sister Bernie was the same. Andi said it was God. Jo said it was his unexplainable good nature. Surely there was a more realistic explanation.

It irritated Daisy that there were religious people who were exceptionally kind surrounding her. She had to reluctantly admit she admired that. She desperately wanted to despise at least something about them. But even Daisy admitted their religion – or their *relationship with God*, which was how Andi put it – was the very last thing that was despicable. It seemed to be a source of strength and comfort. That bothered her… because it didn't make sense.

* * *

15

The car pulled in and spluttered to a halt in front of the shed. A man in a driving jacket, goggles and cap uncurled his long legs from behind the steering wheel. He stretched and peeled off his driving gear and dumped it on the front seat carelessly. He was obviously intimate with the trappings of motor-travel and treated them with familiar contempt. Harry stood at the door of the shed wiping his hands on a rag. He felt it was a shame that spoilt people had no understanding of the value of what they had.

"Can I help you sir," he said amiably. So, this was it: his first real travelling through customer.

"I need fuel and information," he said abruptly.

"Sure. Anything to help."

The man took a comb from his pocket and slicked down his hair. Then he grabbed his small felt fedora out of the car and carefully placed it on his head. He snatched his brown overcoat from the back seat and dug into its pocket. He came over to Harry without any preamble and waved a postcard under his nose. Harry stared at it in shock. The card was the sort that advertised a moving picture theatre. Splashed across the card was the title: *The Daughter of Shiraz*, *starring Lillian Browning... opening soon!*

"You're a salesman then?" he asked casually.

"Hell no," the man said with contempt. "My name's Styles: missing persons... looking for the actress. We thought Lillian Browning was kidnapped or murdered – tragic story – made headlines at the time, but recent details have come to light to suggest she may be still alive."

"Lillian Browning..." said Harry thoughtfully, stalling for time. There was no mistaking the likeness on the postcard, even with the dark Persian hair of a middle-eastern princess. The information being thrown at him sent his mind reeling. Daisy was Lillian Browning... the actress? Of course! He had never been a passionate theatre goer, but even if he was, you don't expect to see your childhood sweetheart on the stage.

"Yeah – she's pretty as hell. Blonde hair... you seen her? Her poor family is so distraught that she's going to miss the Opening Night."

Harry thoughtfully scuffed the dirt. This scumbag obviously embodied every cliché ever invented about the rich, narrow-minded class: indulged, crass, bad-mannered... *and* to top it off – liars. *"Her poor family"* indeed! The man must think he was completely stupid. Harry's fairly tolerant nature bristled. *Well*, thought Harry with annoyance, *I can be just as stupid as you expect.*

"She's got black hair here..." Harry drawled

exaggeratedly pointing to the picture.

"She's an actress – it's a wig."

"I ain't seen anybody 'round here going by that name," he countered.

"She could be going by another name," he said impatiently.

"Could be," agreed Harry slowly, "but how could I say, if we don't know the name?" In the space of three sentences Harry's IQ had visibly dropped by eighty and his mentality slowed to be as thick mud and his sociability became as dense as a brick. "I can help ya with the gasoline though. Got as much as ya need."

* * *

Daisy stood trembling behind the shed with Andi and Jo. "No!" she muttered to herself, swallowing tightly. "No, not now! Tommy if you've sent this man to torment me, I give up. I'm sorry... but I couldn't do better!"

Jo grabbed Daisy by the shoulders and shook her. "Daisy - stop it! Who is this Tommy?"

"Him? Tommy – no... That's not Tommy. He is..." Daisy stared at Jo, dazed for a moment. "He's the Fed," she said finally said. "That's the investigator – he's found me."

"The Federal Police? Now? How – after all this time?" asked Andi.

"I don't know… the court-hearing, I guess. It's all reported."

"Are you going to give yourself up?"

Daisy stared at her. "No way! I'm not going in front of a judge for something I am not guilty of. It's bad enough when the charges are true."

The girls surrounded Daisy in a huddle, and Andi prayed desperately for justice, mercy… and a way out. And both Daisy and Jo didn't even mind.

* * *

The man adjusted his hat and looked suspiciously at Harry who was slowly dragging wooden boxes containing the fuel cans to the car. Harry positioned the funnel, balancing a can in the other hand. It was obvious the man expected him to do the whole thing himself. Harry wiped around the paintwork carefully.

The man came close and held Harry's arm down, menacing. "I saw the way you looked at that picture. Where is she?"

Harry gritted his teeth under the force of his hold. The skin on his arm was still raw and tender, but he didn't wince. He said nothing.

The man brought his other arm up fast and punched Harry hard in the stomach. "Lillian Browning…" He punched again and again. "… where is… she?" he demanded. Harry doubled over winded. Then the man clouted him under the chin. Harry made no move to defend himself. The man's lithe athletic body bounced around him confidently. He reached up from behind and pulled Harry's hair back, his other arm across his neck. "Where is she, bush-boy? Where is Lillian Browning?"

"Let him go. I'm here."

"I knew it," he said smugly, as he gave Harry a shove. Harry stumbled as he wiped blood from his lip with his sleeve. The man turned to face the voice.

Andi stood in her greased smeared coveralls. "Well, what do you want? I'm obviously no longer a missing person, so you've done your job it seems."

He stared at her. "You're not Lillian Browning."

"Why do you say that?"

"You're not even the right age!"

"It is a dangerous thing to accuse an actress of being older than she seems…"

"Your hair…" He was thrown. Would this girl think him stupid? It was so obvious, it was ludicrous!

"Haven't you heard of permanent waves and hair dye, Sir?"

He spun around, kicking up the dirt with his polished shoe and he swore out of frustration. He was so close. He could sense it… he could almost smell her!

He went to grab at her, but suddenly Harry stood between them, and he didn't look like he would stand passively by this time. Styles backed off. "You're not Lillian Browning!" he yelled at her. "It's a federal offence to impersonate a wanted person!"

Andi shrugged. "Prove it."

"What? Are you completely mad? I don't have to prove anything!"

"Well obviously! Otherwise, how could you be ruining my life on no grounds?"

"No one is ruining your life Lillian! What am I saying? You're not even her!"

"How else would I know you're a Federal cop, who has been stalking me – gathering a case against me that has destroyed my career, my life!"

Harry stepped forward. "You're a cop?"

"A Feder... no, I'm not a cop! I'm looking for a missing person... Lillian Browning. How dense are you people?"

"Isn't that police business – missing persons?"

"Oh, give me a break I can arrest you here and now if you don't co-operate!"

"Since you're not law enforcement, that would be a citizen's arrest... for being uncooperative? Really?" asked Andi. She hoped she had stalled long enough for Daisy to get away from the shed and hide inside the house. She didn't know the implications of hiding a wanted person, but in some way, she hoped ignorance would be enough to at least stall the hunt.

"It doesn't take a badge for me to bet on my life that you know her! Where is Lillian Browning?" he repeated forcefully.

"Here," said a voice behind him. He spun around to see a blond-haired figure in the sunlight. The flicker of victory was quickly smothered as he realised there was no other resemblance to the willowy actress. Jo held herself tall as she joined Andi. "She's just protecting me. *I'm* Lillian."

"This school-girl game is not amusing!"

He stopped and stared as Sister Bernie came over to the shed and stood beside the girls. "Is there a problem?" she asked mildly.

"Don't tell me you are Lillian Browning too!" he said with disgust.

Sister Bernie laughed. "Young man – you need your eyes checked if you thought for a second, I could pass as Lillian Browning!"

Harry stood trying to draw everything together in his mind. The missing years... all that time Daisy was gone... she was Lillian Browning – the singer, the actress. "This here is Constable Styles…" The man reddened at the use of low rank, but Harry carried on apparently oblivious to the insult. "He's federal police, and he's looking for an actress going by the name of Lillian Browning," Harry said significantly. "Sister Bernie, you're a highly respected person with your missionary work and all…" He took a deep breath. "Could you help him?" Sister Bernie looked carefully at Harry with raised eyebrows, and Harry nodded.

"Very well then. This way," said Sister Bernie as she sat herself in the front seat of Styles' car and waited. "Son, I can't say I've heard anyone going around town calling themselves Lillian Browning, but we'll soon find out."

Styles looked surprised and then victorious! This was going to be easy after all.

* * *

Sister Bernie set herself on a self-appointed mission to frustrate this man out of town. She could be as patient as a plodding old Clydesdale. They drove all the way out to old Henry and Maud Zimmerlin's place. They stopped when the road ran out and Sister Bernie gathered her hat and strode out comfortably. She told Styles of the treks that she had taken between villages, as a matter of course, during her life in India. The Zimmerlin's ramshackle farmhouse was as old and as unimproved as their pioneer ancestors. Sister Bernie explained this happily devoted couple were the longest living residents of Gum Ridge. It sounded perfectly logical they would be the first choice of questioning. She neglected to mention they were just a little bit senile and a big bit deaf.

Styles picked his way around a bony dog that was chewing on an old cattle shank at the doorway. She knocked loudly and invited herself in. "Henry! Maud! It's Sister Bernie… I've brought an important visitor," she called loudly. "He needs our help!" Maud bustled over to the stove and put on the kettle. She dove into the pantry and extracted some very stale biscuits and put them on a plate. One was growing a fine fuzz of mould and Sister Bernie tossed it to the dog that had followed them inside and sat under the table chewing his bone.

Henry hobbled over and sat down. He smiled a gummy grin delighted to be part of this unexpected company. Sister Bernie continued her loudly amplified explanations. "He's a federal policeman. Federal! Yes. He's looking for a missing actress called Lillian Browning." She paused. "No not atlas… actress – theatre person. Yes – it's true, we've never had a theatre at Gum Ridge. No, I don't think the police will be building one here." Styles quickly summed up the pointlessness of their stay and rose to leave. Sister Bernie didn't flinch. She quickly put her hand firmly on his arm so he sat down once more. She smiled broadly at Maud and spoke quietly, just loud enough for him to clearly hear. "You have to stay and have a cup of tea. It is the price you pay for asking questions. Drink up and smile a lot sir," she said patiently.

The next visit was to Counsellor Penfield. "Counsellor, I would like to introduce you to Agent Styles... Federal Police." The counsellor paled and swallowed hard. "He's looking for an actress by the *name* of Lillian Browning – I told him sir, you would know important names around here."

Penfield swallowed again and he suddenly felt very hot. He began running his fingers around inside his collar. Asking about an actress in Gum Ridge was obviously a front for other work: undercover investigations about taxes perhaps. "No, I don't know the name... a photo perhaps?" The man produced the postcard and the Counsellor studied it briefly. "That's quite a glamour shot for country folk. Browning's not a local name." He urgently wanted to get away. "I have a meeting now – council business. Please excuse me Styles. All the best with your investigation."

Dr Larsen looked at Sister Bernie with the intuition that often occurs between professionals who work well together. "Lillian Browning... I've never treated anyone by that name," he said more to Sister Bernie than the man that sat opposite his desk beside her. The man pushed his point a little, but Dr Larsen just repeated firmly, "I have never treated anyone by that name."

The man patiently endured numerous more cups of tea. Sister Bernie clearly explaining that the Federal investigator was looking for a 'Lillian Browning'. She also mentioned that Councillor Penfield and Dr Larsen and numerous other residents had not been able to recall anyone by that name. Gum Ridge never failed to amaze her. Three weeks ago, this town were itching to lynch Daisy in the street themselves. Today they carefully shut down to the outside. If Lillian was Daisy – or as the case may be... Daisy was Lillian, she was their own to deal with. They didn't need outsiders doing their work.

Sister Bernie had avoided just two places – the hotel and the post office... and she hoped Styles would not notice. But he did. Sister Bernie steered him past the hotel, to the post office. The hotel proprietor would never give any margin of leniency, it was his daughter who had borne the brunt of this humiliation. Sid would be their best chance. She knew Gladys would not be so generous. Her pain was too raw.

* * *

Daisy sat huddled behind the lounge chair in the dark. The curtains were drawn and the dust under her feet felt gritty. She drew her knees up high under her chin, and she held the rag-bodied celluloid doll in a close embrace. Why now? Why – after all this time, when she had tried so hard to shut out the pain? She thought if she paid the price the courts had set – fair and square, it would all go away. Why did the Federal investigator have to find her now?

Daisy closed her eyes and saw the memory of her brother Tommy's handsome eyes laughing from under his slouch-hat. He was so pleased, so young, so passionate. The war gave him a purpose and a mission he never had before. He led others with natural flare. He understood comradeship – that unspoken bond of brotherhood. The irony that *comrade* is a communist term was not lost on Daisy, especially since Tommy was so fervently evangelistic about purging the Red scourge by winning the war. Tommy came into his own. He was promoted and the hierarchy even stalled calling him up for active duty overseas, because he was so valuable in enlisting new recruits at home. He organised Daisy to do charity concerts for the men: to offer them a goodbye and a thank you for serving their country. The concerts were a hit. Lillian Browning was a star. She was beautiful and she could sing, not with a sickly-sweet nightingale voice, but with energy and gusto. The men went wild. They loved her.

After one concert Tommy came backstage to Daisy's tiny caravan. He lay smoking on the lounge in his uniform while she sat and signed a million small cards that said, "With love from Lillian B." He even made her kiss her ruby red lipstick on the back.

"Sis, these will be worth a mint in rations on the front line," he said with a smirk.

"And you'll probably tell them I spotted them in the crowd and wanted you to give this especially from me."

"Never – not unless they're having a really bad day, or there's no mail getting through. The memory of a pretty girl is good for morale, Sis. It's good of you to do this. Real good…" and his eyes spoke volumes of love and respect. That look was imprinted on her memory.

The next concert was when it happened. She was singing the encore, the soldiers enjoying every last moment, when suddenly she stepped into a time lock. Everything went still as she looked at Tommy in the front row, waving his hat in appreciation. She smiled and waved back… this was his last night before he sailed. Finally, he had bulldozed himself into a dispatched regiment. How amazing it was to have Tommy! He was her brother and father and mother and sister. He was all her family rolled into one and he loved her. He'd understood when other people didn't. Tommy was the best!

But as she looked at his neighbour – she realised *that* was Tommy, not the other man. Then she looked further into the crowd, and every face had Tommy's steel grey eyes and larrikin smile. Every face was her brother going to war… and every face may not come back. Somehow, she finished the song and escaped back stage, shaking and crying. Tommy was going away, and she had an awful premonition it was forever.

When Tommy came backstage as he did every concert, she sat pale and drawn, smoking a cigarette with nervous anxiety. "I can't do this anymore Tommy. I can't."

"Sis – the guys love you. This is such a boost for them."

"I just can't." She knew it sounded lame. But she couldn't do it. Not anymore. Not after tonight. It never occurred to her to lie, for just one night, so that Tommy would go away to the war-front secure in his sister's support. This was Tommy. He'd understand.

"It's war Daisy. We all do things we can't, or don't want to. That's what war is. No one ever said it had to be fun." And she noticed that he had dropped the endearing "Sis". He didn't even use her stage name. The look that clouded his face was total disappointment. Of all the people to let down the war effort, he had not expected it to be his own sister. He left then, to go down to the wharf and Daisy never saw him again.

Afterwards, they had written to each other and made-up, but it was a slow and painful reconciliation as an ocean of sea travel between them stalled letters by a world at war. Daisy had not even cried when the telegram came saying that Tommy had been wounded in action. Another telegram arrived soon after, saying in formal military terms that he never made it. In the personal things of Tommy's that came home there was a ruby kissed card covered with mud stains and tears.

"Tommy had not made the *ultimate sacrifice*", thought Daisy bitterly. "Ultimately it was me," because for Tommy there was never a question that his country was entitled to anything less than his life. Daisy valued him far more than he valued himself, and it was her sacrifice to let him go, not his.

True to her word, Daisy never did another concert. She was given offers for large sums of money that a war-torn economy on a shoe-string budget, had no business offering. But she wouldn't budge. She had done her last concert. If she wouldn't do it for Tommy – there was nothing that was incentive enough. In the end she settled their pestering by saying it was due to personal reasons… 'conscientious objection'. According to Mr Jones, that was when the Federal Police had opened her file. She was obviously a communist sympathiser.

Tears rolled down Daisy's face. "Tommy. Tommy.

You know I would never be a communist – not when that is the very thing that stole you away." She had to let him hear. He had to know the accusations were false. But her heart would not stop beating hard. She wanted him to know she was not a coward, that she had worked hard, and she had not chosen the easy way. But Tommy didn't hear, and peace did not come…so she huddled behind the lounge and shed the tears she had never cried to say goodbye.

Gradually the heat of her weeping subsided. "Tommy – you died so I could be free," she whispered. How many times had he told her the reasons why he donned his uniform so proudly? How many times had he preached at her the right to claim freedom?

"But Tommy… we won the war and I'm *still* not free," she whispered to the cobwebs behind the lounge. "I am bound by forces inside of me that I don't understand. You can't shoot at that with a gun and make it go away. You can't fight *this* in a battle."

* * *

Sid stood behind the counter listening to Sister Bernie and looking at the postcard. This was like the hand of God intervening for them, providing an opportunity for justice that they hadn't been able to extract themselves. He knew what Sister Bernie was asking… and he guessed why. Daisy had become her mission field, and even he admitted, it was changing her life. He didn't think it would be perjury if he just said the words Sister Bernie wanted him to say. Gladys joined him staring at the post card in disbelief. Sid quietly held her arm in a silent signal of restraint and asked, "So this is Lillian Browning? What did she do?"

Styles was jack of all the run around. He realized someone, if not everyone knew something. He looked at the traditionalist shopkeeper and the shelves packed with conservative papers and books. He sensed that this was his best chance. "She's under investigation. It's a matter of national security. She's a communist."

Gladys drew a quick breath while Sid quietly looked at the card and tapped it thoughtfully on the counter. "I'll tell you what," he said after a while, "if I ever see a famous actress calling herself Lillian Browning come into my store, I'll be sure to give you the heads up."

When Styles and Sister Bernie left to the quiet tinkle of the little doorbell, Gladys turned on Sid with a hiss. "Sidney! That was Daisy – anyone could see that with their eyes blindfolded. Why would you protect the one person who could take Ruby away? This was perfect! It was the hand of God Almighty!"

"No Glad, that was not God… because it wasn't the truth. That man is on a hunt for a trophy to hang on his wall. Daisy is no more a communist than I am a Tibetan monk."

"But how do you know? She could've got in with any sort of strange crowd in the city… especially if what that card says is true. The theatre is rife with radicals who have no sense of morality."

"Gladys – listen to me. Tommy died fighting it. He was my mate and the most outspoken anti-communist this town ever had. You heard his enlisting speeches. There was no one more against that code. Daisy would never turn to the thing that her brother died fighting. Now I'm not about goin' to start inventing things and calling it the hand of God, just to get my own satisfaction. Whatever she was and whatever she did – she wasn't a Commo. I know that for sure."

* * *

16

Daisy's eyes felt like they had been scalded with acid. She rubbed them with the heel of her hand and massaged the bridge of her nose. In her mind's eye she saw Sister Bernie's kindly creased face smile at her. "God always hears our pain," she had said the other day. Sister Bernie never lectured with long nagging sermons; but she *had* soothed her burns every day and reassured her the scars would fade. Sister Bernie surprised Daisy. She had expected to endure tedious hours of missionary evangelism. But it was only now and then that Sister Bernie would pop something "Jesus" into their conversations… so subtly, so normally, that Daisy hardly even noticed. She would say gentle things like, 'God even gathers our silent tears and keeps them safe'… or, 'He's for you Daisy, never forget that'… 'Jesus will be your peace, and your strength'.

"God? Are you really for me?" In the silence that followed there was a sense of something, tantalizingly near but just out of reach. Where was the peace and the strength Sister Bernie so confidently wore? *"Damn, I need peace! Please God."* Daisy was so tired. Tired of having to be strong all the time, tired of fighting – struggling so hard and still failing. Her pain had a name: failure. In spite of a measure

of success in an industry only a few could attain, it still was not enough. She still had failed.

It occurred to Daisy that if it hadn't been for the investigator that had cut short her ride to the top, something else would have spun her off the merry-go-round. Even if she had reached the very pinnacle of acting success – what then? At some point you come down, and you fail. Then if that was not enough, she realised that she had also failed in something else... life. Ruby. Past relationships, present ones. The lack of internal cohesion stung of deep penetrating failure. Was there no escape?

Tears filled her eyes again. Tentatively she whispered the name that Sister Bernie had so tenaciously used to plant seeds of hope: *Jesus*.

Mysteriously Daisy's heaviness started to float. It lifted and lifted until Daisy couldn't feel it at all. Her limbs felt light and for the first time that she could ever remember, her heart began to smile. Peace – a tangible peace. A peace so real she could hold it, and it rested on her heart. Then a song floated on her lips – not a rowdy, flamboyant stage-show song, but a melody that welled up inside her that wanted to celebrate a budding of life.

Then finally Daisy floated off to sleep... peacefully, no longer afraid in her hiding, no longer condemned in her failure.

* * *

Harry and Sister Bernie had finally said farewell to Styles, smiling amiably through gritted teeth. They did not even bother to look politely disappointed as they waved towards the cloud of dust and smoke that followed him down the road and out of town. Harry turned to Sister Bernie and gave her a hug. "Sister – thank you."

The little lady smiled up at him. "Son – the wind of change is starting to blow."

"Then I expect it will bluster up a storm before long," he said.

Sister Bernie's eyes twinkled as she laughed. "Not a truer word was spoken. But you know what they say about the good Lord: *The winds and the waves obeyed Him.* Just keep praying Harry and it will work out for good."

"I just hope I can accept what God calls a good thing," Harry said soberly as he pulled closed the heavy door to the shed. Sister Bernie looked thoughtful as she watched him mount his saddle horse and ride home.

* * *

"Daisy! Daisy!" Jo and Andi ran through the house. When they found her scrunched up behind the chair, she had already opened her eyes. She was looking thoughtfully at the celluloid doll she held in her arms with a smile on her face.

"The investigator – is he gone?"

"Well, he's driven down the road, so he's gone for now at least."

Daisy sat up and pulled herself onto a chair. She felt so light and it took her a moment to remember why. *God. He was real. He loved her.* She knew this because she was different. The way she looked at the world was different. A bizarre, but irrepressible smile danced on her lips, and she didn't care at all what these people thought about it. "That man should get a Hound Dog Perseverance Award. I have met few who are so dedicated to their work. An actor like that would go far."

Jo and Andi looked at her stunned. What had this person done with Daisy? A cramped, uncomfortable doze behind the lounge did not account for this. The investigator obviously thought he had a good enough lead to spend the entire day talking to people all over town. He could come back with reinforcements to test his theory, but Daisy seemed unperturbed.

Sister Bernie shared a laugh or two with them about some of her investigation experiences over supper. "Mr Harrigan was a classic," she said. "He told me he'd seen someone as pretty as that post-card picture, but who went by a different name. Agent Styles was so relieved he'd finally broken through he almost wet himself! He asked

227

Harrigan many very specific and penetrating questions. Harrigan answered every single one so seriously. He went into a very detailed account of where and how he met this lady and described Daisy down to a tee. He made sure Styles wrote everything down in his note-book. Then Harrigan finally said, "Well, enough of all this – I should just bring her in, since it means so much for you to meet her." Poor Styles nearly had a seizure in anticipation. Then Harrigan introduced Janice! His dear little wife is not at all like you Daisy, although her hair is kind of fair. Harrigan sat there grinning like a lovesick puppy! Lillian Browning! It was the quietest I saw Styles all day. He went quite purple around the ears. I did suggest he should get his heart checked."

As Andi and Jo hooted over the success of their decoy, Daisy went quiet – very quiet. When they looked up Daisy had tears streaming down her cheeks. As she stood, her slight body was trembling. She went over to Sister Bernie. "I can't thank you enough. You didn't have to do this. You could get into a whole lot of trouble…"

"Well, it is apparent an entire town has stood with me," said Sister Bernie softly.

"But that is just it! I don't understand. Is it because they suddenly found out I am - was - Lillian Browning: "The Actress"? Does fame mean so much to them after all?" She shook her head. "If it does - Gum Ridge has changed… a whole lot."

"Fame – here? Sure, there is an element of that. When someone makes it in the public arena – out there, it sort of proves the quality of their roots: here. But I don't think that's it entirely."

"Then what?" asked Andi. She was equally baffled by the events of the afternoon. Each amazing story showed her that nothing in Gum Ridge was predictable, even though it seemed things had stayed the same for decades. Statistically, Styles should have found a dozen takers who would have been delighted to pass on the retribution that Daisy had coming to her.

Sister Bernie looked thoughtful and poured herself another cup of tea. "Perhaps it just seemed like a clever stunt to pull off… and they'd do the same for anyone – regardless of the crime… a bit in the tradition of Ned Kelly: the locals looked after him and he was wanted for murder. Or it could be a Digger-thing perhaps… sticking together in adversity. We are very practiced at that here. Or it might have been aided and abetted by the fact you didn't blab about yourself. It is easier to admire those who don't blow their own trumpet, and plenty are quite willing to knock down those tall poppies who do." Sister Bernie slowly stirred in her sugar with the handle of a fork. "I'm not exactly sure, but don't assume it's over. Defending your own against the outside is quite a different thing to accepting the black sheep who has come home."

"But Harry left town – and I've never seen anyone more accepted," observed Jo.

"Yes, Harry left. But not by choice and he returned whenever he could. Harry's heart is in Gum Ridge. Daisy's ambitions were not. That is an important distinction that they notice."

"But... when I brought Ruby here, I almost signed it in rock that I wouldn't... couldn't come back. And I wouldn't have... except...." Daisy paused. She picked up the doll that sat on the table and stroked its hair into place. Why did she come home? Sometimes she couldn't even remember how it all happened. "Anyway, Styles gave them an easy way out... yet they didn't take it." Daisy's face brimmed with gratitude for the locals who created an unexpected shield around her, even those who despised her.

She suddenly realised she had not specifically asked God for protection, but he had given it anyway. Daisy was the recipient of a generous act of grace, and it touched the very core of her soul. She looked around the room. Something was stirring in her heart. When she spoke, it was as if she was addressing the doll she held in her hands. "I have made peace with God; but I need to make peace with the people in Gum Ridge. I don't know how to do that. Will you help me Sister Bernie?"

Sister Bernie came over and stood before her. She reached out and took the doll from Daisy's hands. "Daisy – you are so courageous to face this. Already your heart tells you it is the right thing to do: to extend the hand of reconciliation. It may not work out the way we would like, but we are responsible just to do our part and let God take care of the rest. It would be my pleasure to stand with you in this. Thank God for His wisdom. He knows things in this situation we cannot begin to imagine."

* * *

Daisy picked up her pen and dipped it again in the inkwell. She had just used the last corner of blotting paper as a drip of ink bled its way up the fibres. In the end she took a fresh sheet of paper and started again. She blew gently on the paper and waited a moment for the ink to dry before she folded the paper and tied it with a strand of coloured wool. Would this simple and uninspiring note encourage people to hear what Reverend McKinley would say, or just promote a full boycott of the whole church service instead? She had never written such a thing before. *I could hardly kiss bright red lipstick onto these notes*, she thought grimly.

She looked into the centre of the vase holding a

bunch of the first everlasting daisies from their garden. She touched some of the flowers, feeling their stiff, papery petals under the pad of her finger. Their centres were a rust colour, tinged with pink. They had been quite excited when the old envelope of flower seeds in the garden tin had turned out to be daisies. These were her flowers. Common daisies… but their paper petals lasting forever. She had chosen Lillian as her acting name because a lily flower is exotic and rare. She wanted to be so different from the plain, common Daisy Ann Brown she had grown up as. *But Lilies only last for a day*, thought Daisy, as she picked the head off a flower in the vase and tied it to the wool around her note with a bow. These invitations were not as ornamental as some she had made for her cocktail parties. This was simple and symbolic. She liked these more. And instead of sealing this note with a kiss, she sealed it with a prayer.

Daisy's stomach churned. She felt like she was about to come out of the dressing room and go on stage. Suddenly she was living her nightmare. The spotlights glared, she was on stage and about to start a song, when she experienced that awful moment again, the moment when she realised, she hadn't got dressed, and she hadn't woken up yet. Only this time she knew it was not a dream. She really was exposed and very vulnerable, and she wouldn't be able to escape until it was over.

* * *

Reverend McKinley looked at his rough hands as he sat behind the pulpit. Pastor's hands are supposed to be soft and gentle, he thought distractedly. His work as a fencing contractor didn't allow for smooth, pastoring hands. Didn't the Apostle Paul tend his trade as a tent-maker to pay his way? Perhaps plying the needle through leather and cloth gave the Pharisee-turned-apostle, calluses also. It was something he hadn't thought about before. He only dwelt on it now, because it distracted him from what was about to come.

The organ wheezed and he stood. He paused and then went and stood in front of the pulpit and took off his robes. Some of the ladies began to murmur behind their gloves as he draped them carefully on the pulpit behind him. Daisy stared at him. What was he doing?

Instead of struggling through a long opening hymn or an even longer prayer, he stood praying silently for wisdom until finally the organ whined into silence. "I know that many of you are wondering why I would change what we always do. Why would I remove the Robes of Ordination? I can only say that I feel very strongly that God has impressed upon me to stand before you, not as a man of 'The Cloth', but as a fellow member of this fellowship. I am stripped of the symbols of authority so that any chasm they may create will be closed. I stand here with nothing to make me special, because in all reality I am just a fellow traveller like you. It is God who gives the authority to minister to each other, not these clothes. They are just coloured cotton after all. Today we have a very significant event to witness. It is important we do it as brothers and sisters in Christ, not as ministers and parishioners, committee members or rostered helpers."

A ripple of murmurings ran up and down the form pews. Jo and Andi sat still as statues. If they had caused a walk out before, what would happen now that Daisy sat with them? McKinley took a breath and continued.

"This week Daisy sent you a letter. It was an invitation and I'm glad you have responded. I would ask if you don't intend to stay, that you leave now, so that we may proceed with what God has laid on our hearts without disruption."

Curiosity was burning like a raging fire. Every eye watched the pastor's face without blinking. The boys stuffed their racing bugs back into their little tin matchboxes. Ladies' hands lay still in their laps; no one was snoring inappropriately. There is no way they were leaving now, before they even found out what was going on. Reverend McKinley nodded thankfully. Not a bottom had moved. He noted that Sid and Gladys were here, but her parents and Ruby were not. He approved of that. The child need not witness the ugliness of offence and frayed tempers, if that's what it came to.

He picked up his Bible and opened it up to John, chapter three. *"Unless a man be born of water and the Spirit, he cannot enter the Kingdom of God,"* he read. "Daisy came to this town as one who was dead. But God has performed a miracle of re-creation. Jesus described this process as being "born again". Daisy is born of water – just like everyone, that is a physical birth. Now she is born of the Spirit – that is the beginning of her spiritual life. Daisy – would you come and stand with me?"

Daisy went and quietly stood beside Reverend McKinley. She was dressed in a simple white frock, and Andi thought she looked stunning. The minister didn't seem to notice. He began to describe the process of God's forgiveness. It is never earned or deserved, but like the woman at the well, it is offered freely to any who would drink the water of eternal life. He turned to her. "Daisy, do you confess before these brothers and sisters in Christ that you believe that Jesus is the Son of God? Do you believe he died on the cross to pay the penalty for your sin, so that you might be spared that punishment in eternity?"

"I do." Her large eyes were soft and full of emotion.

"In obedience to Jesus, you have expressed the desire

to repent for the past, and the sadness you may have caused those present (and those not present), and to extend the hand of fellowship to those who would be willing to accept it? Is this true?"

"Yes – it is."

"Then Daisy, as your brother in Christ, I accept this hand of fellowship," and he turned and shook her hand sincerely. "Any others who would do likewise, I invite you now to come forward."

Harry couldn't get to the front quick enough. He unashamedly strode down the aisle and stuck out his hand. "Welcome home Daisy," he said earnestly. She blushed as she remembered her response the last time, he said that.

"Thank you, Harry. I feel like I am home now."

Mr and Mrs Dunn, Andi, Jo and Sister Bernie lined up behind him. Gradually the pews emptied and the aisle filled as they came to shake Daisy's hand. Last of all were Sid and Gladys. They stood hand in hand before her; every eye was keenly watching. Daisy's face was wet with tears as Sid and Gladys jointly passed their hands to Daisy and they clasped together in a three-way hold.

Daisy's voice was hoarse. "Thank you. Ruby is blessed to have such fine parents. I'm sorry..." she whispered.

Something crumpled in Gladys and she flung her

arms around Daisy. "Oh, Daisy I am so sorry. I was so scared! I thought we would lose her. She is our life!"

Daisy was unable to speak for a long time. She nodded through her tears. "I was scared too. Of different things… but still scared." She paused a moment and then said, "Please – I have a gift for Ruby. May she have it?"

Gladys nodded mutely as Daisy gathered a brown paper package tied up with string from beside Sister Bernie's feet. She pressed the doll-sized parcel into Gladys' arms and whispered, "Thank you. It is the only thing I have ever made that I wanted her to have. It was made out of something that was quite broken and used. That means a lot to me, because now it is something very different. It is useful again. Ruby will not understand this of course, but perhaps you might."

As they returned to their seats holding the parcel carefully, Reverend McKinley dabbed his eyes. "There remains just one more thing to do. Jesus led by example through the waters of baptism. It is a physical symbol of the spiritual event we have witnessed here. Water washes dirt away and God's love cleanses us from our past. We go under the water as the old person and rise again as a new creation."

He took Daisy's arm and led everyone out of the church, down to the creek and the water hole. Together

McKinley and Daisy walked out into the water. "Daisy, on the confession of your faith in Jesus Christ, I baptise you in the name of the Father and the Son and the Holy Ghost." He held her shoulders and dipped her gently under the water.

As she walked to the edge of the creek, Sister Bernie wrapped her in a towel and gave her an enormous hug. "Nothing you have ever given up will compare to what God has in store for you Daisy. God promises that he gives 'pressed down, shaken together and running over'. He crams more blessings into our lives than we can ever contain!"

* * *

17

It was a picnic to die for. The basket lunches were brought out and laid on the tables. Jo stood amazed as the food just kept coming. Laundry baskets reminiscent of a magical pre-war world, became hampers which produced an enticing array of delicious bounty. There were freshly baked bread rolls and roasted chicken pieces that smelt divine, and salads of all kinds. Then there were sweet pastries and pies, cakes and biscuits, and some tasty dried dates filled with sugared cream that the kids would steal off the plates and stuff in their cheeks while their mothers weren't looking. As Jo eyed off the treats, she almost admitted they looked delicious. Almost.

Pastor McKinley stood as he said the blessing. Andi wondered if he would remember to keep it short. He didn't. Even the contagious excitement of a real picnic in the style of the old church anniversaries, was not reason enough to skimp on praying... today.

It had been a long time since the last church picnic. There had been too much stress and not enough grass to make it worthwhile. It was Daisy who suggested this. It was her one sweet childhood memory: the games of cricket and races; the bottomless hampers bursting with goodies;

and the swim in the waterhole before everyone was bundled home tired and ragged.

Daisy laboriously sent out invitations, and organised men to make sure the remaining few prickly pear clumps were cleared from the grass that was returning to the paddocks. She made sure that the toilets were checked for red-back spiders and other livestock. She organised games and co-ordinated the menu so that they didn't end up with fifteen platters of egg sandwiches. Everyone in the district had pinched and saved, dragging out old family favourite recipes. Today was to be really special. Daisy hadn't had so much fun since her very first cocktail party.

It was Sister Bernie who encouraged Daisy to get involved. She knew Daisy was not a behind-the-scenes personality. Sure, she had a lot to learn about this new way of living and Daisy had been doing it Daisy's way a long time. Sister Bernie also knew Daisy needed a place to start and this was as good opportunity as any. Sometimes it seemed to Daisy she wasn't worth such a chance.

Sister Bernie always countered such notions with a story. It was usually a story about using the abilities God had given her with integrity. Sister Bernie was big on emphasising the "integrity" part. "If you can't do a job with responsibility and kindness you might as well go farm fleas!" she would say. "There are plenty of people out there farming their small little pests and the sad part is they think they are managing sheep stations! Do it small, do it right – and you will grow Daisy. When *you* grow – opportunities grow."

At times Daisy thought it was all too hard. Then she wished she could just go away and forget the whole thing. In a way it had been easier when no one liked her and she hadn't understood how God wanted her to live. That would really give Sister Bernie an attack of colic. "You can't go back to Egypt, girl!" she would say with a very firm voice. "You can wander around the wilderness for as long as you like, but it is much better to keep going forward into the Promised Land."

That made no sense at all to Daisy. Andi explained that Sister Bernie was referring to a story in the Bible. The Israelites had been slaves in Egypt. Moses helped the whole lot of them escape their slavery and led them to a good land God had promised would be theirs. Except... the people didn't want to journey through the desert to get there. They became afraid and tired and hungry and cranky. They wanted to go back to Egypt, even if it meant being slaves again. So instead of getting to live in a good place, the people of Israel wandered around in the desert for forty years.

Andi said that even though this story was part of

Israel's history and really happened to the Israelites, it became a time-honoured analogy for the Christian life. "It's like we were slaves, but Jesus freed us. He is teaching us and leading us towards the good plans He has for our future. We can choose to go with Him, or we can go back to our slavery... or we can end up in the middle – not really slaves, but not really free, living in a no-man's land – like the wilderness." Andi said she had heard one preacher say that the whole journey out of Egypt and into the Promised Land should have taken the Israelites eight days... not forty years! If only they hadn't been so stubborn.

That was when Daisy decided she didn't want to be a slave in Egypt – ever again. Daisy could not forget what her life had been like just yet. Living without God was like walking around dead... much worse than even living in a desert. But she didn't want to go sight-seeing in the wilderness either. She wanted to get to the good place God had planned for her... and as quickly as possible.

Flies buzzed lazily around the trestle-tables, under the trees that surrounded the church. Chairs and blankets were scattered together in groups. People said "Amen" in unison as Reverend McKinley finally finished grace and then they filed past the tables loading up their plates. After a hot cuppa tea and enough sweet treats to make their stomachs feel icky, the young and young-at-heart rallied to prove supremacy in the games. Counsellor Penfield was the designated race-caller. There were to be egg and spoon races, sack races, three legged races, a greasy pig chase, and a water tank dunker.

Harry had made up a tank with a seat that collapsed into the water if someone hit the bull's eye target with a ball. Reverend McKinley volunteered to sit on the dunker seat if every ball thrown meant a donation to missionaries. Mission support had never been so high and Reverend McKinley had never been so wet. Even Jo had a go with the ball, and she felt no pangs of guilt as he emerged from the tank spluttering. As he sat once more on the insecure seat, he jovially called, "Put another threepence in the missionary fund folks – this is a once in a lifetime opportunity. The parson gets the dunking – and the parishioners do the baptising!"

He looked affectionately at his slight wife standing in the shade with a spare set of clothes. "I think this is easier than giving a talk before we take up the offering. Perhaps we should keep the tank…" She laughed and shook her head. He looked dubious when he saw the next man step up to the throwing plate. "Perhaps not… I had no idea my brothers and sisters had such a keen eye for staying on target!" he said as once more the seat collapsed and he went catapulting into the tank. Cheers and congratulations erupted as he surfaced again with some strands of green slime hanging off his reddish beard.

Counsellor Penfield started calling the races. The littlies lined up with their teaspoons and their eggs, and mothers stood on the sideline coaxing them on. "POP!" went the cap gun and the kids tore off towards the finish line. More than one child toppled over on the uneven ground and tried to scoop up bits of smashed eggshell and yolk in their spoon to finish the race. In the end only Ruby finished with an unbroken egg – and that was because when she fell, her egg had fallen smack in the middle of a soft cow pad. The cows had been put in the paddock for a few days to get the grass down short. The morning shovel-patrol obviously missed this one. The soft landing had the added bonus that her green-coated egg now stuck to the spoon like glue. Ruby proudly presented her coated egg to Counsellor Penfield who delicately declined to take it. He awarded her prize - a delicious glossy toffee-apple on a stick, made especially for the occasion by Mrs Dunn. Gladys dived in and rescued the apple from becoming smeared by contaminated hands and bundled Ruby off to wash. The competition became fierce when the kids realised there were spoils such as toffee apples at stake.

Jo and Andi went in the sack race. They climbed in the old scratchy wheat bags and pushed their toes down into the bottom corners. The gun went off, and everyone cheered with spur-of-the-moment coaching tips. Andi tried a clever waddle rather than jumping her way to the finish line. She was making good progress until her toe-hold came loose and she ended up head-over-turkey. Jo jumped her heart out and was just beaten by a whisker at the finish line. The winning boy good-naturedly shook hands with his competitors but refused to share his prize apple with anyone.

"The next race is for 'People-who-work-together'. Grab your partner for the three-legged race," Counsellor Penfield announced. Daisy had considered all sorts of categories for this traditional father-and-son race. Since the war, many fathers were absent or unable to race. So rather than abandoned the section altogether, she thought this idea of 'People-who-work-together' was a good substitute. Grandma with Grandson, neighbour with neighbour, uncles and nieces. The boy from the sack race asked to partner Jo. He said she'd made him 'work really hard' for his prize in the previous race so that they qualified to participate. Andi got together with Mrs Dunn. Any loose association of "working together" made them eligible to race. Mr Dunn teamed up with a little boy who stood disappointed on the sideline. "Come on son, I'm sure you've worked with me on a Sunday morning…"

The boy looked delighted and whispered in his ear, "I know you made that up."

Mr Dunn looked shocked. "Really?"

"Yep – we don't work on a Sunday. It's the Sabbath…" The boy chuckled and helped tie their legs together with old stockings.

Harry stood near the starting point as Daisy ran down the line handing out stockings. Couples were practising their timing, and people were laughing as they watched the confused results.

"You haven't been in a race yet Daisy," Harry observed.

"Oh, Harry I'm rather busy."

"I don't have a partner, and… we work together."

"Race? With you? Now?"

Harry shrugged. "We qualify." He tried to make it seem that he really didn't mind one way or the other and was not the slightest bit offended that she thought the idea ridiculous.

She hesitated. "Sure, why not." She grabbed a stocking and firmly tied their legs at the ankles. "You didn't leave much time to practise."

Harry grinned. "We'll just have to learn as we go."

"On your marks… get set… POP!" and off they went.

Jo's partner's name was Bert. They started out at a fully synchronised sprint… and they were over the line and finished while the others were still trying to get started. Jo and Bert were winners! They ran around, arms on each other's shoulders, their legs still tied together waiting for the others to come along. Just to prove their win was pure three-legged skill and no fluke, they tried new challenges like jumping over some of the backless benches from inside the church. Jo suggested they launch a new event – three legged hurdles!

Mismatched sizes and ages and temperaments were taking their toll. Mr Dunn tucked his arm around his little partner's shoulders and hoisted him off the ground and jiggled him along like a tea-bag. Andi and Mrs Dunn were doing quite well – they were just not a team built for speed. "Slow and steady wins the race," puffed Mrs Dunn as they passed another couple sprawled on the grass for the second time. Andi was loath to point out that Jo and her partner didn't take it steady and were the uncontested winners – ages ago.

Harry and Daisy were having terrible trouble. At first it was hilarious fun trying to get a rhythm going: "middle leg; out-side leg", but Daisy was distracted and attempted to go the whole distance without getting too close to Harry. It just wasn't working. It was only Harry's steadying hand that saved them from sprawling headfirst into the remains of Ruby's cow-pat. Daisy muttered in frustration, "I told you this was not a good idea. You should have found someone else."

"I didn't want anyone else Daisy."

"We are never going to make it!"

"There's only one reason that's likely."

"What's that?"

"If you bale out."

"Humph! You sound like Sister Bernie!"

"Sister Bernie's not right about everything you know."

"Well, I haven't found what that might be."

"Middle leg," said Harry firmly. If the truth be known, he was having a marvellous time.

"There must be an easier way!"

"I could pick you up and carry you," suggested Harry.

"No!"

"No?" Harry smirked at the thought.

"Don't even think about it!"

"Too late..."

Daisy stopped dead. "Harry Dunn – I don't mind being your partner, but I am *not* going to be lugged along like a dead weight!"

"Daisy…"

"What!" She flung around to face him and nearly toppled them over.

Harry steadied her by the shoulder. He knew most of their trouble was that Daisy refused to hold onto him or his shirt. "Outside leg…"

"Oh." She blushed and focused, and they bumbled over the line, among the straggling last couples.

"Three cheers for our picnic organiser!" cried Counsellor Penfield. Harry deftly undid their ankle tie and disappeared, while Daisy resumed her duties a little subdued.

The last event was the greasy pig chase. Murray's had donated a little runt weaner – pink and cute… and the prize for this event was the pig itself. Jo was very determined to win the pig to save it from becoming someone's Christmas ham. They poured a stack of oil over the pig's back and then let it loose. Off went the squealing pig followed by a thundering horde of children. The adults laughed as the cornered pig squealed its way straight through the maze of little legs. Bert did a spectacular dive and grabbed it by the back leg, but grease and panic gave it enough opportunity to wriggle free and set off once more. Just to get a hand on the animal was a feat in its own right.

Eventually the little pig began to tire, and the final captor was a girl with pigtails who wrapped him up in her pinafore like a baby and delivered it to Mr Murray. She was declared the winner. It was pretty evident the pig had landed on his feet. The girl soothed and pampered him – feeding him leftovers off her plate. She called him "Murray" in honour of the original owners. Her father was rolling his eyes, saying, "We won't be getting any bacon off that little porker... not if I know my girl. We should've just got her a dog... like she asked." Jo felt better when she over-heard that.

Afternoon tea was served and those who wanted a swim went down to the waterhole, while the rest of the adults tidied and packed up. The sun was getting low and reluctantly families started off home to their evening chores.

    * * *

18

Daisy sat on the stairs of the church with the girls as the evening shadows lengthened. Harry had given someone a lift home and said he'd come back and take them home after he dropped them off. The girls were restless and decided to start walking. It seemed Daisy was not much in the mood for company anyway.

When Harry drove up, Daisy had hardly moved. He got out and sat down beside her. "Congratulations Daisy. You did a fine job."

"Thanks. I'm exhausted."

"It's been a full day."

"In some ways it was like an opening night – the preparation, the energy. In other ways it's better."

"Better than an opening show? That sounds big…"

"In film – you never see your audience. In live theatre, the audience is there, but you never get to know them. Sure, I can read them… and I can play them to get certain responses, but I never wanted to *know* them. It's strange because I know these people. I feel like today has made a difference, and that is new to me."

Harry was quiet for a while. "From what I hear, Lillian Browning made quite a difference. All those concerts for servicemen…"

Daisy was quiet for a long time. She hadn't wanted to think about how the knowledge of her stage career would change things. "One of my directors told me once that his ambition for film was to replicate the impact theatre had on society over and over again. Column reviews are a pretty poor gauge for such things like influence." Daisy paused and sighed. "I'm not sure if I was acting for the audience – or whether I was doing it for me I think it was mostly for me, because when that changed, there was no reason to do it anymore. Perhaps that is what Tommy couldn't understand, because what he did was *always* for the greater cause."

Harry nodded. "Tommy was like that."

Daisy quickly looked to see if Harry was being sarcastic. She still felt protective of her brother. Harry's expression was open and sincere. She relaxed. "Thanks. I know you didn't see eye to eye."

Harry chuckled. "Tommy wanted me to lie about my age so I could join up. I probably would have… except Pa got to me first. He made me swear on my mother's grave that I wouldn't do that. I made some crack about Ma not being dead yet. He clouted me under the ear and told me she would be - if I lied to go to war. It's the only time I remember Pa lifting a hand. The funny thing is, I really believed it was the dishonesty that was upsetting him, not the war. And it might have been, in a way. Pa is not one to shirk one's duty."

"Did you tell him that was why?"

"Tommy? Na. You are right. We saw things differently. I got a few white feathers, even though I wasn't even enlisting age."

Daisy went quiet. The stigma of abandoning the war-effort was terrible. Daisy knew that first-hand. But for a man, to receive a white feather... that was the ultimate shame. Such a label of *cowardice* intimidated many men into enlisting. "Well, I can vouch for you. A coward you are not. I never thanked you for saving my life."

Harry looked at her with a smirk. "I think you abused me for it actually... but you're welcome," he said. He hesitated before continuing. "Daisy..."

"Hmmm...?" Daisy was gazing out over the paddocks. It was good to see the skyline changing. As the cactus was dying, the trees seemed to emerge with fresh life.

Harry felt awkward. "I... well, thank you for going in the race."

Daisy laughed. "Harry Dunn – you are amazing. We came last! How can you thank me for that?"

"Winning isn't everything."

"I was right – you do sound like Sister Bernie. It's

annoying the way she is always right."

"We are not alike at all then – I couldn't be annoying."

"Oh, I'm not so sure about that…"

Harry smiled and stood up. He picked up the last box sitting at Daisy's feet.

"I meant it you know, Sister Bernie isn't right about everything," he said.

"Really – what?"

Suddenly Harry didn't want to pursue it. What if Sister Bernie *was* right? The risks were too high. "Doesn't matter," he said as he rested the box on the back of the cart.

"Oh really? That is such a cop-out," said Daisy. "You know, Sister Bernie has had her fair share of input about you,"

Harry stopped and looked at her. "What did she say?"

"A few things..."

"Like what?"

"Well…like… No – I asked my question first."

"Nope," he muttered with finality, as he finished stowing the box to get ready to leave.

Daisy sensed he was just not going to budge on this. "Obstinate man! You *are* as stubborn as a mule!"

"Sister Bernie said that?"

"No… but I think you are."

"What did *she* say?"

Daisy blushed. "She told me you were solid, God fearing, steady and…. Oh, give me a break! You egotistical individual… you're loving this!"

"Actually, I'm quite relieved… although it makes me sound more like a tank-stand, than something I would aspire to. That's not what she told *me* at all."

Daisy laughed. "Now I'm curious. Sometimes I wonder if you're real – the way people talk you up."

He looked at her evenly. "She said I regarded you out of pity."

Daisy stared at him… and said nothing.

"No clever quip to that?" Harry always felt that Daisy's ability to put things into words left him a little high and dry. He was surprised by her silence.

"I… well, do you?"

"Pity you? No Daisy, I don't believe so."

"Well, what then?"

"I was thinking… love." He smiled in his quiet way and pulled up his sleeves to prove his sincerity. The burnt scars puckered his skin in unnatural waves up his forearms.

"Harry! You can't. I mean – you shouldn't!"

"Oh Daisy, I was prepared to stay back and say nothing… but well, since your baptism and all, I've been so hopeful that..."

"Oh boy." Daisy sat down hard on the step. Harry closed his eyes. Why couldn't he be patient? When he opened his eyes, Daisy's cheeks were wet with tears.

"Oh Daisy – don't. Forget I said anything. Perhaps in time..."

"No Harry. It's not time I need. Nothing will ever change with time."

"Ever?"

"It can't. The past is fixed. I cannot change it."

"I'm not looking to change the past. It's the future that concerns me."

"But Harry – you know about Ruby and the sort of life I lived..."

"This is about Ruby? Why?"

"How could you love me? After all that?"

Harry sat down again on the step. "I've thought about Ruby. A lot. When I found out she was your daughter and you gave her away... I was hurt and angry and jealous. I couldn't understand how you could do that. But do you know what changed my thinking?"

Daisy shook her head. How could she ever face the reality of her decisions? If only she had known then about the courage God gives. Perhaps she would have made better choices.

Harry looked intently at his boots. "I realised you could have decided early on to... you know, stop the pregnancy. No one would have ever known, and your life could have gone on the same. But you didn't. You risked your career and your reputation to give Ruby life. In spite, of everything, you chose to do the hard thing, Daisy. That gave me so much hope. You gave her life and God gave her a family. Glad and Sid didn't know for sure that they were not able to have kids of their own then. God turned a sad situation around and made something good out of it. I believe that baby saved their marriage... their lives..."

"I wish I could go back and change it. I would change so much."

"You said it yourself, Daisy, the past is fixed. But the future isn't. With God's help the future can be better. I know it can."

"Harry, it seems so ugly. How can anyone forgive such a past?"

"What right do I have to hang onto a past that God gave everything to redeem? If I do that – it is saying what Jesus did was not enough... that somehow, I want more. There was no more He could give. Jesus gave everything."

"Oh, Harry – I don't even know how to forgive myself."

"I know how to ask, that's all. God is not one to hold

out on us. You're part of the family now, Daisy. God wants to help. We just have to ask."

"Will you pray for me, Harry?"

Daisy looked surprised when Harry nodded and took his hat in his hands. She hadn't actually meant here and now. She quickly closed her eyes. "Heavenly Father... we know you have forgiven our past. Help Daisy to forgive it as well. And help me to be patient. I know you promise that all things work together for good. Thank you for that. Amen."

Daisy looked up through her tears. "That's it? Just that?"

Harry shrugged. "I just say what I think. He hears."

Daisy smiled through her tears. "Sometimes, Harry Dunn – you are too good to be real."

* * *

Daisy heard the car pull up outside the shed. She wiped her hands and went out to attend to the customer. She stopped dead as she stood face to face with Styles, his driving goggles and cap in hand. He looked at her steadily and smiled. "Hello Miss Browning. I've been looking for you."

Daisy paled. She wanted to run, to hide, to scream, but she couldn't. She stood frozen – unable to move. Styles looked her up and down. There was a smear of charcoal on her chin. "The country life agrees with you Miss Browning. You look well."

Harry called from inside. "Daisy – there's a few of...? I ..." He appeared at the door and was struck dumb as well.

Mr Styles pushed out his hand. "Harry Dunn, I presume. Peter Styles. I believe we have met before." Harry slowly shook his hand – the grease on his palm going all over Styles carefully manicured fingers. If either of them noticed, they gave no indication of it.

Oh boy. Daisy lifted her chin. She took a deep breath. She would stand-up to this. A courage rose inside of her that she had not known before. "Whatever it is you want Mr Styles, get it over and done with."

He smiled out of the corner of his mouth. Harry stepped forward. "Excuse me Daisy, I believe I owe Mr Styles something from his last visit." Harry punched him on the chin and knocked him out cold.

"Harry! What are you doing? Do you want to get arrested for assault?"

"He'll be alright... I'm sure of it." He dragged him by the ankles inside and bailed out a bucket of water from the barrel beside the forge, and slowly tipped it all over him. Styles spluttered and tried to sit up.

"Harry – don't drown him as well!" Daisy grabbed a

towel from a nail on the wall and mopped his face.

"Much obliged, Miss Browning. But it doesn't change why I am here. I have something to give you."

Daisy stepped back in fear as he put his hand inside his jacket. She stared at this man who had hunted her for so long, and suddenly her life was over. Finally, he had won... she was caught helpless. Harry stepped around in front of her protectively. In a moment of transparency, Daisy realised something quite unmistakably. Harry's affection was more than she deserved. *"More than life itself..."* But whoever deserved any of the good things God gave? If God had given her life clarity and purpose, Harry gave it colour. "Oh Harry, I was wrong to put you off. I love you. I know I do," she whispered hoarsely staring at Styles as his hand hovered inside his jacket.

Harry eyed Styles cautiously. He saw a careless, dangerous gleam in his eye. The hound had the scent of blood. Harry was caught defenceless. There was not even anything close at hand to throw. Daisy's doubts rang in his ear. "Does it still bother you that you have a past?" said Harry quietly, his eyes not moving off Styles propped up against the bench in front of them.

She touched his back as he stood in front of her. Would he again prove his love would give everything? "Oh Harry – you know it bothers me. But the future will be better. We can learn as we go."

"And if we fall over, or come in last…?"

"We'll have fun trying. I promise."

"Will you marry me?"

"Oh Harry…" Daisy leant around him and stared at the look on Styles' face. How could she say 'yes' if she was to spend the rest of her life in a prison? He had an arrest warrant in his pocket. Styles seemed amused by her dilemma.

"Just answer the fellow, will you? I've got places to be," he muttered adjusting his position more comfortably and continuing to finger the inside of his jacket.

This was so unfair. Why couldn't she be what Harry deserved? "Yes," she whispered.

"I don't think he heard you, Lillian."

"Yes – I will," she said definitely. She could retract it later if she was sent to prison. Right now,… in this moment, she needed to reassure him of her love.

Styles laughed and struggled to his feet. "Congratulations to the happy couple." He pulled out a wet, soggy envelope from his pocket and passed it to Daisy. She recoiled as if he had handed her a viper.

"You have to open it now. I can't leave until you do."

Reluctantly Daisy went over to the bench and

carefully peeled back the envelope and unfolded the wet paper. The ink had run but was still readable. She looked up in surprise. "Mr Styles, I don't understand. What is this?"

"It is an invitation for Lillian Browning and four family members or friends to attend the opening screening of *The Daughter of Shiraz.*"

"It's not a warrant for my arrest?"

"Doesn't look like it. I'm not a Federal agent anymore Miss Browning – I got a better offer."

"But you've trailed me solidly for five years to prove my anti-nationalist sympathies. Can you give up just like that?"

"Miss Browning, you misunderstand me completely. I have no personal convictions on matters of Federal policy. It is true I don't like losing – but the war is over, and I'm keen to move on, that is all." He wobbled slightly and rubbing his chin. "The producers approached me to find you, because they knew I was their best chance. Their remuneration was somewhat healthier than a policeman's wage… and there's an attractive bonus if you attend the screening. They are of the opinion that a gala event without the star is missing something. So here I am."

"But if she goes – they could arrest her anyway." said Harry.

"The case was tentative at best. The clean-up from the war-office has higher priorities... I doubt anything would stick. Don't know many who care so much anymore. Besides, I saw the way this town rallied. It's not only movie audiences who love Lillian Browning," said Styles.

Daisy smiled. He didn't need to know that nothing could be further from the truth. It was plain Daisy Brown whom they had accepted – with her chequered past and scandalous failings. Most people from Gum Ridge had not even heard of Lillian Browning until Styles came searching for her. Daisy Brown was the household name here, and only in connection with a church picnic. And for Daisy, that was an abundant unexpected blessing.

* * *

19

Doctor Larsen lent Harry his car for the occasion. Andi, Jo and Sister Bernie sat in the back seat cramped and uncomfortable, as they bounced and jolted all the way to the city. The metal trunk strapped to the tail-gate held their going-out clothes.

"But Daisy – how can the movie be released when you didn't finish filming? You were only halfway through the movie when we left…" Jo had tried to work this out. She knew Daisy had staged her disappearance during the shooting of the film. Had they substituted another actress?

"They don't shoot scenes consecutively. I told them I wasn't happy with the chase-scene and wanted a re-shoot. The director was humouring me. He said he had everything he needed."

"The filming was finished?"

"I had a contract to fulfil… I couldn't just bail out. Every roll of film is money. To leave in the middle would mean they'd have to re-shoot the whole lot with another actress. But at the same time my disappearance had to look like it was not set-up…"

Andi laughed outright. "So now she has a conscience! Why were you so hard to motivate when the contract was for renting a roof over our heads?"

Daisy glanced sideways at Harry. He seemed to be concentrating hard on driving over the rough wagon rutted road. But there was a suspicious twist of a grin playing around his lips.

"So, we will actually get to find out how the story ends. Does Shahnaz escape and find a way to be a modern princess?" asked Andi.

Daisy looked mysterious. "You will have to wait and see…"

Andi groaned. "That is *sooo* unfair. After all we've gone through – we should be able to have an inside hint on how it ends."

* * *

They had dressed in their hotel rooms and were ushered into the theatre on a red carpet. Everything in the theatre looked bright and fresh, muted with candle-light ambience. A string quartet hummed softly in the foyer as the guests of honour arrived. The ladies flounced with beads and feathers and the men looked polished and suave in their suits and bowties.

Journalist flashed their large box cameras and asked Daisy about her puzzling disappearance and sudden re-emergence into public life. She smiled gracefully and posed for the photographs… her long eyelashes working overtime for effect. She answered their questions, leaving out a few minor details – like Gum Ridge and the Federal headhunt.

The organ played softly as the Master of Ceremonies welcomed the guests. Waiters walked around with trays of champagne and platters of gourmet delicacies. Harry went quieter and quieter, until he found it hard to breathe, and excused himself. He had to go outside for some fresh air. Jo nodded to Andi and they followed him out. "So – how does it feel to be engaged to the illustrious actress Lillian Browning?"

Harry took some slow deep breaths. "I can't get used to it. I'm engaged to Daisy. This Lillian Browning hardly seems like the same person."

Jo thumped him on the back good-naturedly. "I've got news for you buddy – they are the same person. And like it or not, you are marrying Lillian too."

Harry blinked and swallowed hard. All this glitz and palaver was a whole world away from Gum Ridge. Andi bounced restlessly on her toes. "Hate to break up a deep heart to heart here guys… but we are missing the party and they are starting to go in to take their seats." Harry didn't move, so Andi tugged impatiently on his sleeve. "Come on. I don't want to miss this!"

Harry sighed and reluctantly followed the girls inside.

An usher met them and guided them officially down the aisle. As they walked, the other guests, cast and officials stood and clapped Lillian all the way to her seat of honour in the front row. Sister Bernie looked about in amazement. "I don't remember the last time I was in a theatre."

The organ made a flamboyant introduction as the captions flashed up, framed by date palms and rolling sand dunes. Lillian burst into the palace garden dressed in her filmy Persian dancing costume. Harry's eyebrows shot up. The audience clapped and cheered. She fluttered her eyelashes in distress and the audience was with her one hundred percent. Any quest she pursued, any challenge she encountered, they would be there for her. The scene blanked out and the caption filled the screen: "Mother, I honour my father - the King. But I need an education before I marry!", and the audience erupted in cheers. This was the modern way to live. Ambition with purpose! Andi could see it was far more than mere entertainment. This reflected their ideals.

The audience hissed the villainous fiancé and cheered beautiful Princess Shahnaz in her search to fulfil her aspirations and find true love and happiness. As the Princess came out of the theatre dressing rooms, ready to practice her stage dances – she glows with the memory of the handsome, romantic Antonio. The organ growls a warning, and Princess Shahnaz sees the slight flutter of fabric alerting her to the ugly henchmen lurking there.

The audience erupts as she flees, and the chase begins. The organ accompanied the panic and chaos with precision. Jo and Andi looked around; eyes wide in amazement as they saw people standing up cheering her on. Ladies adorned in glamorous evening-wear were yelling out warnings to Shahnaz on the screen without any inhibitions. When Shahnaz sees her beloved Antonio tied up, but is powerless to help him, the audience hushes in suspense, and then erupts in malicious laughter as a villain slips and is buried under a pile of collapsing scaffolding and curtains.

The organ resumes its hasty crescendos as Shahnaz takes advantage of the chaos and runs out onto the stage and down the centre aisle of the theatre! Andi held her breath, and instinctively reached out to hold Daisy's hand. She turned and looked at Andi and Jo, smiling in the flickering blue light of the silver screen. The film rolls on. Shahnaz runs out onto the street. As she dashes around the corner with the villains in hot pursuit, the screen blanks out. Intermission.

"They've got to be joking!" scoffed Jo in disgust. "They just leave people dangling to sip drinks and make small talk! What a way to kill a moment!"

"I'm kind of relieved," said Andi. "We are passed

the moment where we came in. it means we'll get to see the end of the movie. I thought that maybe…"

"Really?" said Jo looking at Andi with her eye-brows raised. "Andi – the movie is as corny as. It doesn't stack against classics like Star Wars!"

"Jo that is so unfair. It's not meant to. It's kind of… well an innocent cameo of good versus evil… love versus hate… success versus failure. The basic battles in life. That's all most movies are anyway – when you get down to it."

"Ooooh, and who made you film-critic of the century? And that would be *last century* – in case you've forgotten!" said Jo sarcastically. She looked around. She felt incredibly displaced. She wanted to go to a real theatre with real popcorn and real junk food; and watch real plots with real special effects… and super-real surround-sound.

"I'm just going to the dressing rooms to freshen up," said Daisy. "Are you girls okay?"

"Sure," said Andi before Jo could say anything. Harry escorted Daisy out the back. And Andi resumed absorbing observation of the clusters of people that milled around sipping more drinks that were served by waiters. They were exclaiming with delight over the story and the set and the actors' performances, and the miracle of moving pictures. No one seemed the slightest bit miffed that the suspense had been broken. For Jo, it was violating a golden rule of movie-experiences.

* * *

"So, what do you think?" asked Daisy shyly as she powdered her face in front of the mirror, looking at Harry's reflection. It was suddenly very important what Harry thought.

"Oh Daisy – you're great." He hesitated and then almost blurted out, "I'm not sure it's right though!"

Daisy blinked. She had not expected him to be so frank. Her heart sank. When she chose to disappear, she never expected to be able to share her part in this movie with anyone. Now she wanted Harry to take pleasure in her success. "Really – you think it is wrong?" She sighed. "Well, it's done Harry – I can't undo this either."

He stared at her for a moment as she painted her lips with a fine brush. "Oh Daisy, no! I don't mean that. You were wonderful. I mean… well…" Harry struggled to put into words the emotions that filled him as he looked at her. "Daisy, God has given you a very special talent – a gift. I'm not sure it's right that I should ask you to marry me. We don't even have a theatre in Gum Ridge. Perhaps you were right to leave. I wonder if Lillian is more of who you are than Daisy… and I hardly know her. It breaks my heart, but Daisy if this is what you would like… if this is what you need to do... you should do it."

Daisy looked intently at his reflection in the mirror. His face was grim and sincere, and traced in sadness. "Harry – you mean that, don't you? Do you think that God could use even this?"

"Of course, he would use it. And, and, yes, I mean it. I don't want to hold you back from being who God created you to be... or doing what He has called you to do. If this is it, Lillian..." He shrugged resigned; his eyes sad.

Daisy stared at her painted nails. "Called? This is a calling? I would not have thought that possible. I thought that maybe this was just my selfish ambition..."

"Selfish depends on who it is for. I have always thought that when we commit our way to God... he plants ambitions in us. It doesn't have to be an expectation that God wants us to do the things we don't like. He made us the way we are."

She paused then and swivelled in her chair and faced him. "And what about you?"

He shrugged. "I have the shed."

"But no helpers..."

"Andy and Jo maybe. I'll get some. Not like unemployment doesn't exist." He shrugged. This hardly seemed important. Not when...

"Harry. This is me. Daisy. I'm still me! My feelings

haven't changed. I didn't stop wanting to be an actress, just because I started to love you. And I won't stop loving you, because those things are still part of me."

"But how? This is an impossible situation. Gum Ridge is no place for an actress."

"I thought that once too. That is why I left. But it is a wonderful home for Mr and Mrs Dunn. Harry, I don't know if I'll ever have another audition accepted to work on a movie. It is a fickle business. You don't know how unpredictable! Once that stressed me enormously and I had to be everything that *they* wanted so I wouldn't miss out. Now? I don't mind so much. If God opens up doors for me to work again in movies, I would love the opportunity. If He doesn't, I'm not unemployed… I have other things I can do. They might want the picnic to be an annual event. We might be able to open a theatre in Gum Ridge. They have talked about one for as long as I can remember."

Harry stared at her, his face melting into a boyish grin. "Seriously?"

Daisy stood up. "Harry Dunn, sometimes you are too good to be true. Once, to have my name in lights was all I wanted. Now my ambitions go far beyond the screen. I want to be a wife, and God willing – a mother, a real mother this time. I want to be known as a reliable friend, and a person that makes a difference in our community.

Harry – once I thought such things were small and narrow. Now they seem so priceless to me… rare and beautiful."

Harry's gaze lingered on Daisy's reflection. "To find a virtuous wife – her worth is far above rubies[ii]," he quoted quietly.

She blinked and glanced at the ring on her finger. "What?"

"It's how the Bible describes you, well – it describes a wife … 'valuable, far above the worth of rubies'."

"Really? It says Rubies? They are my favourite."

"I remember when we were kids, you used to talk about becoming famous so you could wear jewellery made of rubies. I wasn't at all surprised at Ruby's name. It was so like you. If I ever had any doubts, she was your daughter – her name alone confirmed it."

"So… nothing has changed after all. Rubies are still my ambition!" Daisy stood up and hooked her hand in Harry's arm and led him back out to see the end of the movie.

* * *

20

Andi and Jo sat down and waited for the movie to restart. The lights dimmed and the curtain reopened. The organist started running his fingers up and down the keys in a crescendo. Princess Shahnaz ran down the street and fled into a Chinese junk shop. The villains had lost her trail and stood looking about old Chinatown, confused.

A flash back to the theatre shows the bound director struggling to free himself. Would Antonio be too late to save his princess?

Princess Shahnaz peeks out the balcony window and her dark moustached villainous fiancé spots her and points. "There she is!" the caption read. They rush into the shop, knocking things this way and that as they dash up the stairs. The Chinese shopkeeper chases them waving an oriental vase over his head, his long-plaited pigtail flapping dramatically. Cornered, Princess Shahnaz climbs out over the balcony and balances on the balustrade in an attempt to get away. She looks around desperately. There is no escape.

Her fiancé smiles his greasy smile and holds out his hand to the Princess. "Come away with me my love. Our kingdom awaits us." The audience boos and hisses in contempt.

Princess Shahnaz stares at the narrow street below. "No! I would rather die than be your wife!"

The villain turns ugly and snarls. The caption flashes: "So be it!" The audience starts throwing things at the screen, hissing and booing violently. As he lunges at Princess Shahnaz, the Chinese shop-keeper bursts out onto the balcony and hits him on the head with the vase. The villain slumps to the ground.

The deputy henchman looks bewildered for a moment and then bravely challenges the old Chinaman. He ties the poor old man up (with a rope that just happens to be lying there), then he steps forward with a leer. "The King will reward the return of his daughter with her hand in marriage... and half his kingdom!"

Princess Shahnaz shakes her head. "Never!" With dignity she prepares to jump off the balcony. The henchman grabs her arm as she leaps and holds her captive, dangling precariously high above the stone street below. Just then Antonio, the director, arrives. He beats up the remaining henchmen and releases the Chinaman who flees. He goes to inflict a fatal blow to the deputy villain by launching him over the balcony, when he hears his beloved call from below. Killing the villain will destroy his princess. He can see their grip slipping. Quickly Antonio grabs the rope and ties it to the balcony and around his chest. He climbs over the edge and suspended by the rope; he grabs Princess Shahnaz around the waist just as her hold finally gives way.

The villainous henchman, in one final vengeful attempt to destroy the Princess, gnaws through the rope with a blunt knife. Antonio quickly starts swinging on the rope. He creates enough momentum to swing Shahnaz and himself through the window of the apartment below the balcony. They smash through the window, as the rope finally snaps through. As they pick themselves up out of shattered splinters of glass, the villain bursts through the door with a Chinese sword and challenges Antonio to a duel. He grabs a poker from the fireplace and skilfully defends his love... around and around the dining room table. Antonio, in a comedy of errors, becomes entangled in the rope that saved his love from certain death. The villain quickly places the sword to his chest. "The princess will marry me. Do you have any last words before you die?"

Antonio smiles. "Watch out?"

The villain is not fooled. He will not fall for such an ordinary ploy. Princess Shahnaz comes up behind and hits him over the head with a casserole. The audience cheers her bravery. The china dish smashes, and noodles go everywhere. Antonio takes a taste... "Too good to waste on a coward! Bellissima!"

While the police come and take him away, Princess Shahnaz is delivered a letter. She is offered a job in the diplomatic service as ambassador. She faints with excitement. In the closing scene Princess Shahnaz and Antonio dance a slow waltz in the fading sunset outside their theatre. They are now safe from bankruptcy. "The show will go on!"

The audience claps as the lights are raised dimly. There is a quiet, sort of satisfied hush as people seem to want to linger in the moment. Jo kept her head down and covered her eyes with her hand as people got up to leave. She just hoped that Daisy wouldn't ask her what she honestly thought. *I am probably not the kind of person who can lie just to make her feel good about herself,* Jo confessed to herself with a smirk. She glanced over at Andi. She sat starry eyed, still staring at the curtains that were closing slowly over the screen.

"Excuse me... we are closing the theatre now. Can you make your way to the foyer?" Andi focused. The guy from the box office was standing there with a torch.

"Sure." It seemed that now the movie was over, so were the festivities.

Jo's heel on her shoe caught on a loose thread in the carpet, as they came out into the light of the foyer. There was a distinct lack of opening night pizzazz. A dusty cabinet held an old movie projector, a few posters showed other Lillian Browning movies that would be screening during the film festival.

Andi stared. Film Festival? They stood momentarily stunned, blankly trying to adjust their thinking. The 1920's was just another decade in history and they were no longer friends to the frustrating and glamorous Daisy.

Jo burst out into a grin. "Yes!" she exclaimed.

"What are you so happy about?"

"I don't have to tell Daisy I hated her film! And we can go and eat some serious junk food at a real movie!"

"Jo! How can you be thinking about junk food… after all that?"

"I am in serious chocolate withdrawals. Come on – let's go and get a shake. Anything is good."

They wandered out onto the street. Late night shoppers roamed around looking to pick up a bargain. They went into a coffee shop and ordered milk-shakes and a piece of chocolate cheesecake to share. They sat down at the tables on the side-walk and watched the people go by while they waited for their drinks.

Finally, Andi said, "If I could do that again, I would change one thing…"

Jo glanced up as the waitress delivered their tray. She bobbed her straw up and down, delectably enjoying the feel of ice-cream floating on top with shavings of chocolate. "I'd really change the plot of the movie."

"Jo – stop it. It was not that bad. I still think it was kind of innocent." Andi scowled. "I would change… well, it, kind of sounds stupid…"

"Can't be worse than the movie. Okay. Tell me, what *you* would change?"

"Well, I think I would try to be more understanding – before we knew how the story would end. The people story I mean – not the movie story." Jo raised her fair eyebrows as Andi continued. "We were lucky – we got to see the ending… pretty much anyway. But I think hardest thing is to be understanding, even though we might never know the end of the story. Life is not really like a movie – we don't get a chance to film another take of a scene."

Jo continued dipping her straw. She hadn't actually drunk any of it yet… she just wanted to enjoy the anticipation. "That's true enough. We only get one shot at it."

Andi nodded. "That's exactly what I mean."

"I think Harry was really good at it giving his best go, first go."

"Can you believe Harry never said anything to Daisy about being in his house?" Andi said with a laugh. "I cringe when I think of what I said about that dump! It was all true... but not very kind. He never said anything about that either."

"There's a lot about Harry that was different to the rest of Gum Ridge. But I liked him a lot," said Jo. "Even when we didn't get it right, he made you want to keep trying." She picked up her glass and took a long drink. "This is delicious!"

"Maybe it is important to keep trying... and to help others to keep trying. Daisy almost gave up, but she didn't. I'm glad about that. Did you see the way she looked when she came back from intermission with Harry?"

Jo laughed. "I've never seen Harry look so out of water, but he was there for Daisy... and she was so proud of him!"

"I thought she would, well – be a bit ashamed to show off her country friends to the show-biz world. She was so ambitious! I liked what Sister Bernie said about ambitions being given by God... and we just have to keep them pointed in the right direction."

"Huh," said Jo as she finally slurped the bottom of her drink with the straw. Was this the answer? Was God really okay with personal ambitions? If that was the case... what personal ambitions would he give her? She choked on the thought. Was God really that interested in her? It hardly seemed like it was possible to have a custom-Jo-sized ambition that was just for her. How would she even start a dreaming a dream like that? "Well, I know I don't want to be an actress… and I don't want to be a black-smith come motor mechanic… or a shop-keeper or a farmer or a cook. I wonder if there is a dream that is just right – just for me?"

Andi picked up her fork and took another piece of cheesecake. "Sure, there is. My Mum says God lets us know by 'passionate energy'… we know by what inspires our heart. Out of all the things that happened, what stirred you most?"

Jo grimaced. "Not fire-fighting! When I grow up, I don't want to be a fire-man."

"Me neither!"

"Or house renovator!"

"Right behind you there."

"Or nursing…

"Then what?"

Jo paused. "Ruby," she said finally. "Kids… little kids like Ruby. Ruby had a good family – but there are plenty who don't. I'd like to help them."

Andi looked at her. "Even if it gets messy?"

Jo nodded. "Yep – I guess so."

Andi pushed the cheesecake over to Jo. She was just a bit envious that Jo was suddenly so clear about her ambitions. "See, there you go. You do have ambitions…

precious ones – like Ruby! I think that's cool." She frowned and finished her drink. Huh. But what about her? Andi could say God had it all sorted, but when you're sitting at a table on the sidewalk and everyone else seems to have a clear dream, and you don't… that doesn't seem so neat. Passionate energy? Nothing like that stirred her at all. Wasn't she the one who always prayed and was always trying to do the right thing, and helping others? Why would God make it clear for Jo when she wasn't even sure she believed in God? Why would she not even have a clue about something this important? Why would God hold out on her? Why couldn't she have a dream? There were just too many 'whys'.

Jo finished off the cake and gathered up the crumbs from the plate as if she was savouring the last of the idea a little bit longer. "Yeah. Kids. I'd like that." She looked around carefully. "But for now, my ambitions are reduced to getting out of these clothes before someone I know sees me!"

Andi pushed aside her serious thoughts and smothered them in a laugh. "Hey! And you said you would never dress up in 20's gear – not even for your very best friend!"

"Yeah, well… around you Andi, I'm learning to *never* say 'never'!"

More Stories by Olwyn Harris

Gems of Australia: 6 Part Faith Series

#1 Sapphires of Hope

A tacky basket that is the only thing available for Andi to use as for her catering assignment reveals some interesting pieces of historical information. In order to try and understand what they mean, Jo and Andi visit the farm where the basket came from with June, a distant family member, but find themselves in the circumstances that almost cost Andi her life and almost destroyed the livelihood of the family living at the time of our Federation. Jo learns that having hope enables people to keep going even when things are beyond your control.

Houses of Healing Series

#1 The Beachside Cottage

Eliza-Beth finds herself being disowned by her family and in danger of being sent to the poorhouse. Jensen, whose heart is still broken by the sudden death of his wife, meets Eliza-Beth on a dark night and devises a plan to rescue her from her impending doom. The journey they embark on leads them to where neither of them expected to end up.

#2 Petrea Downs

The death of her husband leaves Meg struggling to keep the farm going on her own. When she shoots a stranger, who is trying to steal her cattle and is required to nurse him back to health, she has no idea that Ben Harker is going to be the salve needed for healing her own deep-seated wounds of grief.

#3 The Writer's Retreat

Tess, a romance writer, prides herself on letting her characters tell their own story. When she arrives at Rocky Creek B&B, the run-down stone cottage looks like the perfect place for her to retreat to, not only to write her book, but to escape her past. As she discovers her characters and explores their stories, she finds that God is intent on becoming part of her own story at the same time. As her relationship with the local publican challenges her to stop running, she realises that real life, and real relationships can be messy and complicated. Can she honestly confront the ugly aspects in her own story, so that God can bring them both to a place of healing?

Matt's Boys of Wattle Creek.

When Matthew Lawson's three sons were born, he wrote each of them a letter outlining his hopes and prayers for their futures. When he decided to give up his city job and move to the little town of Wattle Creek, he could never have imagined the effect it would have on his young family. As Matt's boys grow to maturity and find their places in their community, will his dreams and prayers come to fulfilment? Will his boys develop their own faith in the eternal God? And will they each find the kind of love that Matt holds for his beautiful Josie?

Maggie & Minotaur

Another great book by this author. Maggie & Minotaur is a conflict-filled journey to the earlier days of Australia's colonisation. A time when racism and classism was rampant. This book uses historically accurate and yet, very confrontational language, especially around the issue of race, words we don't use in polite society these days. It paints an accurate - if unflattering - picture of early life in Australia. All that aside, however, this book takes you into the home and lives of a very culturally diverse society trying to come to terms with the changing expectations of the time, woven through with wonderful characters, loving relationships, and the ever-present grace of God. Olwyn Harris knows how to tell a story and this book is no exception!

Coming Soon from Olwyn Harris

Gems of Australia: 6 Part Faith Series
#3 Emerald Dreams
Another journey finds Jo and Andi back in colonial times and they are horrified at the living conditions of most of those who had no choice but the live in Australia.

Children's Stories

Bush Olympics
A great story that helps children understand that they are unique in God's sight and that if they work with the skills that He has given them they will be able to work as part of a team to achieve great things.

[i]The Bible passage: 2 Kings 5, tells the full story of Naaman.
[ii]Proverbs 31:10

Lightning Source UK Ltd.
Milton Keynes UK
UKHW010626040221
378234UK00001B/269